ANTIQUES
TO DIE FOR

AN ISLAND COZY MYSTERY

PEYTON STONE

Peyton
Stone

PEYTON STONE BOOKS

CONTENTS

1

— ı —

CHAPTER 1

"Sometimes I think I hear voices in my head. I've always believed it was God, but now I have doubts. I am not satisfied with my life as is, but rather the satisfaction of doing what is right is what drives me. The night is dark for those who remain silent in the face of injustice. This is the beginning of my work." The Killer.

***

"The withered flower,

    deceiving of one's own self,

    justice blooms for them."

"This is a haiku, right, Jax?" Lola asked her twin brother as she took her eyes off the bold headline and the photo of the note in the local newspaper. It apparently had been left at the crime scene like a cryptic warning, or message. The story of the haiku leaving murderer took up several pages of the local newspaper.

"Yes, sister, it is. The killer doesn't seem to be a dim-witted person, huh?" Jax replied, seemingly impressed with the killer's skill.

They sat on the bed in their aunt's old house above the antique shop in Jaramillo, the village where they had grown up. She decided to return after getting the call about her aunt's death and her suitcases were sitting in the room, unpacked.

While Jax had inherited their parent's beautiful home on the outskirts of the village, Lola was now the owner of the antique shop with a quaint and roomy loft on top. Her struggling career as a writer in the big city left her more than ready for a new start. It helped to inherit a more secure, (and profitable) business like that of her late aunt. She was *almost* a little too thankful for the news of her passing. The twins virtually had no relationship with their aunt, but they were her only living relatives and Lola was the only one left to inherit the last of their family's estate on the island.

Jaramillo was the perfect place to unwind, start over, and enjoy life. It was a charming island village with very few inhabitants, yet, the tourists were like swarming bees once winter hit on the mainland. The always-perfect weather invites a person to let their sorrows melt away under the sun's rays - and, coincidentally, the perfect place to commit a murder.

Jax continued, "At the salon, the ladies talk nonstop about nothing else, you know?" Rolling his eyes, he grabbed some of Lola's clothes out of the case, sniffing them. "The old ladies propose theories about who the murderer might be based on the haiku. They also keep chatting about some detective that will arrive in a few days. Apparently, the local cops are stumped," Jax mumbled after making a face and tossing the shirt back into the suitcase. "Since I started working at the salon three years ago," Jax huffed, messing with other garments in the suitcase, "after another bust with my book, it's like I'm the island's therapist or something," Jax groaned, collapsing on the bed next to the now half-empty suitcase.

"And who do the ladies at the hair salon suspect?" asked Lola, grinning ear to ear as she grabbed her most coveted crochet bag and placed it on the dresser. *What should I start on next?* She pondered...gazing at the bright orange yarn ball, its strands hanging over the side of the worn-out beige tote.

I want you to take me there, Lola. Nobody scratches under my ears like those ladies. I hope they don't bring any poodle dogs... added her cat Jade, manifesting as a voice in Lola's head as she sauntered into the bedroom with the twins. Jax paid the pure white, silky, long-haired Siamese cat no mind. Lola, on the other hand, gave her a puzzled look as she made brief eye-contact with her. That cat says the darndest things...

Jax, unaware of Jade's interruption, continued, "The dead guy is Daniel Smith. The cabby who brought you home the day before yesterday. Do you remember?"

Lola remembered and nodded somberly, slightly pausing with the shirt that Jax had sniffed before putting it into the drawer. Two days ago, Daniel had driven her to Jax's house and they had had a brief, yet enlightened, conversation about unique crochet stitches. She vaguely remembered seeing a taxi driver's identification card on the back of the driver's seat that had said, Daniel. It was eerie that he was now dead.

"Yeah, the ladies at the salon, especially Janet- she used to be mom's piano teacher- she would not stop going on and on about Daniel getting with his best friend's wife after they divorced last month," Jax continued, flopping his hands on the bed like a petulant child.

Lola stopped unpacking, faced her brother with curious, wide green eyes. "Sooo, who are they saying might be the killer, Jax?" Lola whispered.

"They think it might be poor heartbroken Richard," Jax replied, sitting up on his elbows to meet her gaze with his own set of matching green eyes. "If you didn't notice, the haiku also speaks of betrayal. Of course," he slumps back, "the police will suspect him first, I'm sure of it. Although, there's something that doesn't quite add up for me," he concluded cryptically.

"What doesn't?" asked Lola, intrigued by her brother's words, returning to unpacking her swimsuits.

"Richard was interested in writing. I know because we met at the writing club on Tuesdays. I know, I know," Jax sighed after Lola jerked her head around to glare at him, a piece of unruly auburn-streaked hair catching in her eyelash at her sudden motion.

"He was terrible, Lola. I can't imagine him writing a complex haiku. Richard was more into writing action stories or fantasies with dragons and stuff like that," Jax replied, shaking his head in disbelief folding his arms over his forehead.

Dragons? The fire-breathing long dogs you've shown me in your books? Interrupted Jade.

Lola smiled and shook her head at the feline's amusing inquiry. Jax quirked an eyebrow, peeking at her from under his arm, then over at the white cat now eyeballing the orange strands of yarn from the top of the mahogany dresser. Though Jax didn't hear what was so funny, he imagined that Jade had made one of her strange comments to Lola.

"Well, I guess you would know, Jax, you've been here longer than me," Lola replied as she tucked the flyaway strand behind her ear and finished unpacking the last of her things, tossing her flip flops at the foot of the bed. "Oh, did I tell you that I'm making you a sweater? I'm crocheting it, which isn't easy so I expect praises when I'm done," Lola grinned haughtily and flashed her emerald eyes, through a wink.

"Yes yes, I will sing of your praises, dear sister. I guess I could really use a sweater this fall anyway," Jax grunted as he sat fully erect, stretching his arms overhead. "It actually gets chilly at night here on the island," Jax confirmed, smiling kindly as he stood to hug his sister.

Jade finally gave in and swatted at the teasing orange strand, easily snagging the fibers in a single swift motion. Her black-tipped tail darted back and forth in triumph. *I like poems.*

***

The next morning, though the murder still plagued her mind, Lola decided to focus on her new life and got ready to tackle her new business venture.

Why a haiku? She thought before shaking her head.

Getting dressed in a lovely but casual green-blue, wispy island skirt and a simple yet sophisticated gray-blue tank, Lola takes a second glance in the Cheval mirror. *Crap... I think I look like a tourist*, she thought. *Oh well, here goes nothing.* Unlocking the door leading down to the antique shop, she descended the 1860's original spiral staircase, thinking. *Today is the day...the shop is officially open under new ownership.* Taking a deep breath, she pulled open the door at the bottom of the staircase, ready to meet the employees Aunt Elena had briefly mentioned in the will. One condition of her inheritance was that they were *not* to be fired.

The morning sun shone through the back door's stained glass Calla Lily, as Lola closed the door to her loft behind her. At that moment, Lola felt a rush of optimism, remembering the sun on her face as a young girl, walking down the narrow hallway to the main shop. She had always liked antiques. They had a charm and mystery that sparked her imagination; objects with an untold past but bound to one's future. They were fascinating, telling their own stories when she needed inspiration for her writing, which Lola still dabbled in when her hands weren't occupied by crochet hooks.

Okay, Girl, let's do this. She took a deep breath, opened the door with a smile and walked into the store. The antique shop was larger than she remembered. Five small rooms filled with furniture, paintings, books, jewelry, clocks, lamps, and other curiosities. The main foyer held a fine crystal glass case that was etched and lined with hammered gold and silver. The large 1820 register looked ornate and still worked.

Lola felt like she had entered a hidden treasure cove. She remembered tracing the curves of the precious metal framing the edges of the glass, going around and around as her parents did business in the back. The treasure was the memories flooding her senses and the riches contained therein were hers to protect.

"Hello?" she shouted.

"Who is it?" an impatient-sounding voice responded from one of the side offices, tucked back behind the main room.

Lola followed the voice and found a young man sitting at a desk, working on a computer. He had dark sandy, cropped hair and square glasses that were definitely too big for his face, but his nose held it up like a champ. He was wearing a faded black t-shirt with the logo of some music group. He turned toward Lola and exhaled heavily, seemingly annoyed at Lola's presence. He made a point of looking at the time on the Lenzkirch Meerjungfrau German Wall Clock, not seeming to notice that someone was in the shop with the front door still locked.

"Hello," Lola said cheerfully. "I'm Lola. I'm...I'm Elena's niece and the new owner of the shop," Lola stammered, fidgeting slightly with her hands. As she continued to meet his unwavering gaze, she repeated, "I'm the niece of Elena."

The young man frowned, "Yes, I heard you, but...that can't be."

Shifting her weight onto one leg, dropping her hands at her side, "Well, hi to you too, but, yes, it can," Lola retorted, taken aback by the young man's direct and unpleasant tone. "I inherited this shop from my aunt Elena, I finalized the paperwork week's ago with the lawyers. That makes this my shop," Lola confirmed, shifting her weight back to the other leg, standing firm.

"Your aunt?" He questioned, placing an elbow on the desk and leaning forward towards her.

"Yes, that's what I've been saying. My aunt, Elena. Is there an echo in here?" She replied, slightly exasperated that he seemed to have zero clue about her and what had happened since Elena passed.

The young man shook his head. "That can't be true." He repeated.

"And why not, pray tell?" Lola put her hands on her hips, now curious, but also slightly annoyed. This man was clearly out of the loop, but did he have to be so rude this early in the morning?

"Because I work here and no one told me that my boss would be…" motioning with his hand up and down, "someone like you…much less the niece of Ms. Elena," the man grumbled as he stood with a deep sigh.

Lola blinked her darkening, yet questioning emerald eyes, "Really?"

"Yes," he said impatiently with a dismissive wave of his hand. "Whatever the case, I'm Brandon Smith. I've been working here for two years as Ms. Elena's online seller."

Lola remembered that her aunt had mentioned something about hiring someone to help her with online sales.

"Ah," she said. "Well… nice to meet you." Lola tried to add some enthusiasm and softness back to her voice - extending her hand as she stepped forward toward Brandon.

Brandon didn't seem to share her enthusiasm as he spoke again, ignoring her friendly tone and hand. "And… what are you going to do now?" he asked suspiciously, adjusting his glasses and crossing his arms. Though his voice was solid, his frame was lanky and thin - he really didn't look all that formidable.

Lola shrugged. "I don't know... run this place?"

Brandon snorted. "Yeah, right," he said, dropping his arms and adjusting his large glasses again. Apparently, his nose had given up on keeping them in place.

Lola could clearly see that Brandon was not happy with her arrival. She stepped back and wondered if he had some kind of agreement with her aunt that she was unaware of. She decided to try to be polite anyway...after all, he couldn't be fired...unfortunately.

"What do you mean by that?" She asked, crossing her arms and shifting her feet once again, standing her own ground at nearly 6 inches shorter than his 6'1.

Brandon rolled his eyes, "I mean you don't seem like someone who knows anything about antiques," he said matter-of-factly. He sat back down as if he already had the upper hand and didn't have to *prove* himself to her.

Lola bristled and snapped, "That's not true," she bit her tongue and reigned in her annoyance. "I've always liked antiques. I think they have a lot of history and beauty," Lola gestured toward the lovely German clock.

Brandon scoffed, "History and beauty? That's not what sells, lady. What sells is rarity and quality. And you have to know how to find them, appraise them, and market them to those who are avid collectors. Do you have experience in that?" Brandon questioned, taking off his glasses completely, looking up at her with piercing brown eyes from under sandy brown eyebrows.

Lola hesitated, taking another step back, feeling slightly embarrassed. "Well... no. But I'm willing to learn," she finally replied.

"Who is here Brandon? A customer?" A chipper voice called out behind her.

A slightly older man, with a tired yet friendly face and a name tag that read 'Charles' approached them.

He stood in the door frame and exclaimed, "Ahh! You must be Lola! Jax said you would be coming by!" Charles announced happily.

"She is..." Brandon started.

"Happy to be here!" Lola quickly interjected, "My aunt left me this business when she passed," Lola completed with a broad smile as she quickly turned around to greet Charles. Her skirt spun around like a school-girl's skirt.

"We are happy you are here, aren't *we*, Brandon?" asked Charles, who seemed genuinely happy to see her, glancing over at Brandon - hoping he would catch on and share in the enthusiasm.

He didn't oblige. His glare, the swinging glasses in his hand, and his tone towards Lola wasn't moved one bit by Charle's intervention.

As the uncomfortable silence continued, Charles stammered, "I..I see you've met Brandon, Ms. Lola. He's as friendly as a porcupine and as respectful as a burp, but I assure you he's a good guy, " Charles chuckled nervously, trying to lighten the mood.

Lola giggled at the comment. Brandon frowned in disapproval and slid his glasses back on. "Don't trust Charles. He's a slacker who only knows how to joke. He has no idea about antiques either," he grumbled, turning his attention back to the computer.

Charles shrugged. "It's true, I have no idea. But I like being here, surrounded by dusty old things. They remind me of my grandmother." His broad smile lightened Lola's mood almost instantly.

She smiled back. "And what's your position here?"

"Well...anything, really. I helped your aunt move boxes, clean the back rooms, and attend to customers, especially when we're packed with tourists," Charles explained, walking back out of the doorway and into the hallway to allow Lola to pass.

"Customers? What customers? This business is dead!" Brandon growled after them.

Lola sighed, *what a pessimist Brandon is. Why can't I fire him again?* she mused. Ignoring him, she whispered to Charles, who stood just a head taller than her, "I'm sure we can revive it. We just need a little creativity and enthusiasm."

She made her way to the front counter with Charles to get more familiar with the business and far away from Brandon. Turning back to her new employee she asked, "So, where do we start?"

"An old typewriter came in yesterday and we have no idea how much to appraise it for.... The guy who sold it to me wanted to get rid of it, pronto." Charles replied with a reluctant sigh and shake of his head, pointing to the beautiful piece on the back counter.

She took a deep breath in and slowly released the air between her teeth. Between learning about the business, Brandon's grumpiness, and this beautiful typewriter, Lola wasn't sure where to begin...she hadn't even had coffee yet.

Turning towards Charles, "That's where I need your help," Lola stated, "I need your guidance, your experience, your advice...and maybe Brandon's too because we clearly both don't know what we're doing."

Charles smiled cheekily, "As sure as I can write poems and serenade a young maiden... I am at your service," Charles took a deep bow as chills ran up Lola's spine.

***

A few days later, business seemed to be picking up. Despite the uneasy, chilling feeling Lola felt before, she's kept her cool around Charles. There's no way he meant anything by that or that he could possibly be the murderer...after all, that was just absurd, wasn't it?

The three of them had cleaned up, sorted out what was to be displayed in the ornate glass case, the separate rooms, and how to keep up with online marketing and sales. Once they came to an understanding of the shop's operations, which Brandon begrudgingly agreed to, they were ready for the tourist season to begin.

Lola was polishing and cleaning the old typewriter in another back office when she heard the front door of the shop slam violently as an agitated voice cut through the air.

"Brandon," growled a man, "come here! We need to talk." It was an older man's voice, deep and chilling; it came into the store like a gust of wind, wounding the spring day.

Lola got up from her desk and cautiously made her way to the front. As she opened the partially closed door to the main room, she saw Brandon coming out of the back room with a scowl on his face. He clearly knew who this man was by the way he didn't hesitate to confront him. She vaguely recognized him too, once she got past the deepened wrinkles, sagging jowls, and thinning peppered hair...he was Randall, the owner of the downtown bar where she used to have a drink with her friends before moving to the mainland 10 years ago.

"What do you want?" asked Brandon bluntly, meeting him just at the threshold of the shop.

"I need some money. I'm going through a tough time and I need a thousand dollars," said Randall with an imperious tone, slightly shaking.

"Money? Seriously?" Scoffed Brandon. "You come here and demand money...you've got some nerve," sneered Brandon, starting to turn away from him.

"Be a good son. You *owe* me," growled Randall, reaching toward Brandon.

"Don't you dare call me son!" Brandon snapped back. "You're not my *father*," he spat, eyeing him up and down, "You... pfft, you're not. You're just a sperm donor," quipped Brandon, stepping away from a now red-faced Randall.

What the rat's nest?? Jade peeked her head between Lola and the door after hearing all of the commotions, her curious eyes gleaming a vivid green and narrowing vertically.

Lola stepped back uneasily, unsure of what to do. She debated calling for Jax; this could get out of control real fast by the look on Randall's face. Jax said he was coming by, but he didn't say when, and Charles had the day off.

"You little bastard!" Randall spittled angrily, stepping closer to Brandon.

Lola, move!!

Lola grabbed her head in pain and fell through the door. Almost instantly, Jax caught her from behind as Jade let out a piercing yowl and dashed between Lola's legs. Once Jax broke her fall and sat her on the floor, he immediately rushed over to the two men and grabbed a hold of Brandon.

Damn he's fast, how did I not see him coming? Lola huddled against the wall of the room, hair standing on end and her breathing rapid.

"STOP! Get out of here!" Jax shouted at Randall. It was clear he had underestimated how strong Brandon was despite being so tall and lanky; Jax could barely hold him back.

Lola was paralyzed at the sight in front of her. Her head felt as if it was going to split. She looked over at Jade who didn't return her gaze but was clearly agitated. Lola groaned, shocked by the immediate pain and the commotion in front of her.

Brandon stood at the ready, breathing heavily and clenching his fists, allowing Jax to hold him as he watched his father's eyes dart back and forth between him, Lola, and Jax.

"You don't make enough money anyway working in this dump," Randall spat, turned around and charged through the front door, nearly knocking it off its hinges.

Lola, get up. It's death. It's him.

Lola pushed a strand of hair behind her ear, looked at Jade who was casually licking her paw and washing her face, and then looked back at her brother and Brandon. Her pain was gone. She pushed herself off the floor, walked to the two men, and cautiously put a hand on her brother's shoulder.

"Jax, Brandon...are you okay?" she asked softly.

Death. Like a dead mouse.

Brandon turned to Lola and his eyes filled with a mixture of anger and pain. "No, I'm not okay. How could I be? That man has ruined my life," he said bitterly, shaking off Jax's grip.

"I'm so sorry, Brandon, about your father," Lola said sympathetically.

"He's not my father. He's a monster," Brandon sneered, with disdain.

"Do you want to talk about it? Maybe it will help you to vent," Lola offered.

Death. Jade had moved next to the front counter and glass display. Calm. Cool. Her pure white tail with a black tip, swishing back and forth, holding Lola's gaze. *I could use a squirrel right now.*

Lola's stomach growled. Loudly.

"There's nothing to talk about," Brandon scoffed, looking at her stomach, "I just want to forget him and move on with my life," he snapped. Shaking his head, he headed back to his office, muttering, "Get something to eat already, geez, I couldn't talk to you anyway with all of that noise."

Lola's cheeks flushed. Goodness Jade!

Jade, who innocently jumped up on the counter, looked at them curiously and meowed.

"Hey, Jade," Jax greeted her, scratching her ears.

Jade jumped off the counter and trotted off after Brandon, catching up to his ankles for a good rub before disappearing with him down the hall.

I'll follow death like a mouse after cheese. I want to tell you that man is a bad guy. Stay away from him, Jade warned.

Why do you say that? Do you know something about him? Lola asked, startled.

Bad intentions. Hunger. Death. I smell it on his breath, Jade hissed with disgust.

"Poor Brandon," Jax muttered once he was out of earshot. "His father was trying to reconnect from what I heard. Apparently, it's not going well."

All Lola could think about was Jade's last hissing words: *Hunger. Death. I smell it on his breath.*

2

— ◆ —

CHAPTER 2

After Randall's untimely visit, Lola and Charles put in a heavier, reinforced, door. To keep it welcoming to new customers, she added wind chimes with stained glass Calla Lilies. She had hoped it would improve Brandon's constant sour mood. It didn't. Charles at least didn't mind it and agreed it would add some lightheartedness to the shop. He was worried after hearing about the incident with Randall.

The withered flower,
deceiving of one's own self,
justice blooms for them.
The withered flower,
deceiving of one's own self,
justice blooms for them.
The withered flower,
deceiving of one's own self,
justice blooms for them.
...with a side of tunafish and cream.

Lola looked up from counting the money in the register, startled by Jade's voice and even more disturbed by her repeat of the haiku murder poem. Jade was seemingly asleep, nestled in the seat of a child-sized

Pardoll Antique Chair against the front window that was adorned by curtains of linen with an amber hue. She looked peaceful there, basking in the soft morning light. The black tip of Lola's tail, however, was twitching. As Lola leaned forward and looked closer, her tail was in sync with the haiku syllable pattern.*Twitch Twitch Twitch Twitch Twitch - pause - Twitch Twitch Twitch Twitch Twitch Twitch Twitch - Pause - Twitch Twitch Twitch Twitch Twitch: The wi-thered flow-er, de-cei-ving of one's own self, jus-tice blooms for them.*

Lola gasped at the sound of the shop door opening, yanking her out of the luring and hypnotic rhythm of the haiku Jade was strumming with her tail's pitch-black tip.

"Hello, Miss?"

Lola blinked twice, shaking her head, the haiku, still a faint whisper in her thoughts. "Yes, tunafish, please," she groggily muttered.

"Sorry?" the man asked, puzzled by her words.

Lola felt like she was coming out of a trance. When she looked up, the man was right in front of her...tall, dark, dressed in a suit and red tie. He was actually quite handsome. "I-I'm so, so sorry, I was, uh, yes," Lola stammered, "um, may I help you, sir?"

The man stared at Lola before turning his attention to Jade. "Beautiful cat. It's quite amazing that you both have the same emerald eyes. Fascinating." He seemed to be deep in thought as his eyes darted between the two before he shook his head. "Sorry, good morning miss. My name is Marco, and I'm interested in seeing your antiques."

Lola slowly stood up from sitting on the Antique Victorian Swivel Stool, puzzled by his question, "What exactly are you looking for? Are you a collector?"

"Yes. I'm intrigued by all sorts of rare commodities," he casually said, tapping on the glass countertop with his free hand. Lola noticed he was carrying a briefcase in the other. Besides his formal appearance and distractingly good looks, Lola couldn't help but notice he was tall, broad-shouldered, and impeccably dressed. His sandy blond hair was styled in a classic side-part, and his chiseled jawline was accentuated by a few days' worth of stubble. Clear blue eyes scanned hers with a mix of confidence and intensity.

You need a boyfriend...but not this one. He's hairless.

"Uhm," Lola cleared her throat to mask the surprised gasp that tried to escape, turning her head down so he wouldn't see the slight flushing of her cheeks. *Don't embarrass me like that Jade!*

"Of course, please take a look," said Lola, motioning to some of the more valuable collections in the ornate glass case his hand was on. He reached up, took off his sunglasses and looked at Lola, meeting her gaze when she briefly made eye contact, before taking a closer look at the objects in the case.

Lola was captivated by his blue eyes and intense gaze - even if it was only for a whisper of a moment. She felt a flutter in her stomach, and Jade made a loud hairball sound.

"Thank you very much for your kindness," said Marco, smiling with his white and perfect teeth after looking curiously at the cat. "Is that...cat, okay?"

"Yeah, yes, um, yes, she's fine," Lola waved off, returning the smile. *Rude.*

"Is anything here that catches your eye?"

He glanced back up. "I'm mostly interested in antiquities related to history and literature. I'm a big fan of Japanese historical books of the 17th Century and handwritten letters."

"Then you're in luck," Lola exclaimed, leaving the counter and going towards the back center room. "We have a varied collection of international historical books, including a selection of books on

Eastern culture. We also have some fascinating historical documents and poems in our library collection."

"Really? Can you show them to me? I hadn't thought to ask for poetry."

Lola froze. "Oh, I must've mistaken you for another customer," she lied. Though she attempted to avoid meeting the stranger's eyes, she couldn't help but realize how much he was paying attention to her. She thought she sounded like a rambling fool. "Right this way," she continued. Lola led him to an enclosed bookshelf within the dimly lit room, perfect for setting the mood to appreciate the historic relics, where she kept the antique books.

Jade stretched, not happy to be disturbed but deciding to follow them, stretching each leg and waking up her limbs.

After Lola handed him some cloth gloves on the mantle, the stranger set his briefcase down back behind him, out of sight. Carefully handling the fragile books, she showed him some rare items from the collections contained within the glass bookcases and shared their origin and value while setting them on the adjacent Lord Raffles Console Table.

Marco was seemingly very interested and asked her several questions about the authors and some of the meanings behind the writings. "You're quite the expert on the subject," Marco complimented her. "I'm surprised you have so much knowledge about each of these books."

"She doesn't, half was what she's saying isn't true," murmured Brandon from the doorway.

Lola, Lola, Lola... the cat said in a playful tone. *Don't you realize who this man is?*

Lola looked for Jade with her eyes, finding her sitting at Brandon's feet. She tried to glare at the cat, but Jade was staring beyond Marco's

legs, her tail, twitching. Then she snapped her head at Brandon, realizing what he said. He was standing in the doorframe, arms crossed
over his t-shirt, hiding yet another music band logo, leaning against
the door frame looking rather smug. With *her* cat next to him no less.

She felt her face flush with heat before turning to apologize to her
new customer, but instead of eyeing Lola, he seemed to be sizing up
the stranger in the room. In the same way, Jade mimicked the motion
as well, her tail still once more.

What? What are you talking about? Lola replied to Jade as she
glared at Brandon.

Marco interrupted the inaudible conversation. "Excuse me? And
who might you be?" Marco's eyes narrowed at Brandon, but his
awareness and body language were towards Lola, taking a step back
away from her.

"I'm the guy who actually knows antiques and categorized every
single piece in this room," Brandon boasted as he uncrossed his arms
and made a sweeping gesture. He had a smirk on his thin lips, as he
admired his work. "Okay, okay," Brandon continued, twirling around,
"she's not *lying*...but I must say that *I*, dear sir, can certainly assist you.
When it comes to the written word of history, I am the expert here."
Lola thought he was about to take a bow after that performance. She
crossed her arms, rolling her eyes.

Show off.

Jade sauntered slowly around the stranger, sitting just in front of
the hidden briefcase.

"Miss Lola here," Brandon gestured, "only recently came into the
antique business...just before that untimely murder, now that I think
about it," Brandon said, standing directly in front of the stranger,

hands on hips, nearly eye to eye and nose to nose. "So, she's not the expert you want to see, it's me."

The man cocked an eyebrow, and shook his head, but he didn't back down. Instead, he crossed his arms over his chest, the white gloves a stark contrast to his dark suit, and with authority stated, "I got what I needed. Thank you though."

"Wait, what, really?!" Brandon huffed incredulously, dropping his arms and slouching. "But, I..." his jaw clenched, and Lola half expected him to start flopping on the floor like a 3-year old who just found out they can't buy the toy they wanted. He must have been incredibly embarrassed, especially after his grand entrance.

Brandon faced Lola, stood upright again.

Lola caught herself forming a slight smirk and cocked her own auburn-colored eyebrow before biting her cheek to prevent the smirk from growing. "Brandon, it's okay, I got this," she finally managed to say.

"I'm going on lunch, then" Brandon grunted, though it sounded squeakier than he probably intended, "Don't call me for 90 minutes...I've got more exquisite books to appraise," he said more confidently, eyeing the stranger one last time before turning on his heels. In just three long strides, he was out the door and Lola just knew there'd be a conversation about it later.

Marco looked at her again after Brandon's brief interruption, uncrossing his arms.

This man is not a simple customer. He's a detective. He came to snoop...just like a poodle who smells butts all day; they never stop.

Marco's mouth was moving in her direction, but Jade's words blocked out the world for a second. It took her a moment to realize she was staring at the mysterious stranger with a big goofy smile.

When she saw a flicker of unease in his gaze, she caught herself and quickly pursed her lips together. Taken aback by Jade's comments, she took a moment to take in his entire presence: a nice suit, yes, but not new, pressed, but not crisp and, was that a stain on the lapel? And his cologne was subtle but pleasant. Nothing screamed detective to her.

Lola glanced down at Jade, perplexed. *What? How do you know that?*

By his smell. He smells like burnt wood.

Lola looked at her cat again, who was standing absolutely still on Marco's right, far enough back to not quite enter the man's field of vision. *If you were a human, your behavior would be so strange,* Lola told her cat.

A vision came to Lola like a hologram in front of her. It was clear that she was seeing through Jade's eyes as the cat looked right at the briefcase. Marco Rossi - Detective was etched in small lettering at the top of the briefcase. *Show off.*

"Miss, are you listening to me?" Marco asked, a forced smile on his face.

Even when he's trying to fake it...it's kind of creepy, yet...cute, Lola mused.

His smile is like the roadkill I picked up this morning...rubbery and stuck to his teeth, Jade corrected.

Shut up Jade, Lola snapped, quickly placing her hand over her mouth and running her fingers back through her hair to conceal her reaction.

"I'm sorry, what did you say to me?" Lola managed to say once she put a straight face back on. She blinked, and the world returned to normal.

"Could you recommend any poetry books, perhaps from Asian descent, Japanese to be more exact? It wasn't exactly what I was looking for, but my curiosity has been piqued and you seem to be just the person to quench it. Since you mentioned poems earlier," Marco replied while looking at Lola.

What is he really doing here, Lola thought to Jade, her eyes narrowing at the detective.

"Poems, Miss?" he asked again, ignoring her inquisitive look.

Lola didn't know what to say. "I'm sorry I'm so distracted," Lola shook her head, a strand of hair falling onto her lashes. "I'm not sure if I can recommend any Asian poetry, it's not my specialty. But I'm an amateur writer and literature enthusiast, so I can recommend other books. Have you read *The Daughter of Time,* by Josephine Tey? The famous crime novelist that published her book in 1951?" Lola asked, closing a book and quickly placing it back in its place, while directing her gaze to another pile of books stacked on another shelf. She pushed a strand of hair back, avoiding his gaze as she removed her white gloves.

Immediately, she realized she hadn't been subtle enough. A suspicious person like a detective wouldn't easily be fooled by her ploy to avoid talking about Japanese poetry. Plus, he would be wary of her recommendation of a crime novel. He was going to realize that she's trying to avoid the poems. *Crap,* she thought, squeezing her eyes shut.

Marco narrowed his blue eyes. His once relaxed posture tensed a little. It wasn't noticeable to the naked eye, but there was a change in air for sure.

Instinctively, Lola's gaze strayed for a very brief moment, landing on Marco's briefcase, but it was enough for the man to realize that she knew he wasn't really there for the antiquities. Marco gave her a resigned smile. Though he didn't know *how* she could know, it was clear that he knew she did.

Lola understood the man's smile and decided to ask him directly. "What really brought you to my store?" Lola asked, leaving behind the mask of a friendly salesperson to reveal the face of someone who wanted answers. She finally had a chance to dive deep into the antique world and share what she's truly learned, taking on the role of an antique shop owner, and this guy, *Mar-co,* wasn't really interested after all.

Marco's smile shifted and became serious for a moment. "Oh, I see you've noticed. I confess, my presence here is not coincidental," Marco turned back to the case of books, running his white-gloved finger along the spine of a rather ornate cover. "I can't say any more about my purpose, however." He turned his head to her and for a few seconds his deep blue eyes and her green ones met, competing to see which one would look away first. It was Lola.

"I don't see how I can hel-"

"I'll take this," he quickly cut in. In his gloved hand was the only copy the shop had of The Naked and The Dead by Norman Mailer. Though it wasn't one that needed to be handled with such care, the price said otherwise.

Jade meowed.

After officially introducing himself via his American Express card, he said goodbye to Lola, assuring her that they would see each other again soon.

Be careful with him, Lola, cautioned Jade as soon as Marco left, walking across the glass countertop.

Why? she asked silently, not that she had any reason to since they were now alone.

He has a horse face, the cat grimaced, licking Lola's fingertips with her rough tongue.

Lola couldn't help but bust out a snort-laugh.

And he smells like lies. Lots of lies. Lies he has told and lies he will tell. He smells like a lie as if he's been soaking in it.

Lola stopped laughing. Proud of herself, Jade started purring.

3

—·—

CHAPTER 3

H ours after the encounter with Marco, Lola still couldn't get the mysterious man off her mind. Her legs were tired as she trudged up the spiral staircase, the steps feeling like they had doubled since this morning. On the other side of the door to her home were her friends, Cristina, Lucy, and Andrea. She had arranged to meet them at the end of the working day, and they had come in earlier through the backdoor of the shop, where the Calla Lilies graced their beauty. As children, the four were inseparable, which lasted all the way through high school. Unfortunately, they lost touch when Lola moved to the city. Now that she had returned to their hometown, they were more than ready to catch up on their lives.

Lola felt a renewed sense of energy. Even though Marco still lingered in her thoughts, it was time to have some girl talk. She took a deep, refreshing breath, taking in the familiar scent of the heavy oak door, then headed inside to greet her childhood friends, now all grown up.

Cristina gasped in awe, "Wow, you look stunning Lola!" she said as she finally saw her longtime friend come in the door.

Lola bashfully tucked a strand of hair behind her ear and blushed at the compliment before closing and locking the door behind her.

"Look at you," Cristina whistled. " How sophisticated you've gotten!" she added with admiration, pursing her lips.

"Pssh," Lola scoffed without thinking, eyes gleaming as she saw her friends, crossing the threshold into the living room where they were waiting. Everyone seemed to have stayed the same, as if frozen in time. She gestured around and continued, "It's been ten years since I left and how come none of you have changed a bit?"

Andrea shot up from the plush black loveseat and instantly smothered her in a hug, sobbing. "Oh my gosh, I've missed you!" she cried. She was almost a half foot shorter than Lola but her hug was like that of a bear

Lola returned the affection, wrapping her arms around her dear friend placing her cheek on Andrea's black hair, "I've missed you too," she whispered, overcome by the sudden emotions choking her up. Andrea was still the same... the lovey-dovey, emotional, yet sassy one!

Lucy, who was never really a hugger, flashed her a peace-sign and a wink, tears welling up in her hazel eyes. That's all Lola needed; her besties were back in her life.

**

The four of them chatted around the hexagonal, frosted table, savoring their coffee and tea around a meat and cheese charcuterie board and a delectable looking chocolate pound cake. Andrea, after freshening up, eagerly shared about her latest beau and was met with howls of laughter as she went into detail about her boyfriend's strange sleeping positions. "I can't believe it!" she exclaimed, gesturing wildly, "I found him upside down, wedged between his bed and the wall." The group laughed out loud as they imagined it - Andrea had a small bed, after all. "He was completely unconscious! I had to shake him for five minutes to get him to wake up," Andrea choked, reliving the moment.

Lucy chuckled and took a sip of her mint tea. "I can relate to that," she said, twirling a finger around the rim of her mug after setting it down on the matching coasters, swirled with clouds with embedded flecks of jade. "My cats sleep in the weirdest places. One time I found one of them sleeping in a pot that was hanging on the wall. And the other one likes to curl up in my boots when I'm not looking." The group erupted in laughter as they imagined Lucy's cats curled up in her boots - blood red stiletto boots to be exact.

Cristina turned to Lola. They were both sitting on the Persian rug that Lola had found in one of the store rooms and Cristina had just popped an olive in her mouth. Leaning forward, her hand on Lola's, she asked, "So when did you get a cat? Especially a cat like that," she asked, pointing towards the kitchen where Jade was sitting, looking regal and surreal. Her fur almost appeared to be glowing, accentuating her emerald eyes and black-tipped tail even more.

In unison, the other two women turned to see Jade, a small gasp escaping their lips upon seeing the unusual feline.

Jade blinked slowly.

Lola hesitated and a hush of anticipation fell over the room. She hadn't even realized it was the first time she had thought of or sensed Jade since seeing her friends again. She looked around the room, slightly anxious she hadn't noticed Jade, or in this case the lack of Jade, before now.

"It was two years ago. I was walking back to my apartment and I heard this pitiful cry," Lola started, looking fondly at Jade, "I followed the cry and saw her, wet, scared, and hungry. Boy she looked rough!" Lola giggled.

Jade yawned.

"I couldn't just leave her," Lola continued, "She let me pick her up and take her home. I had no idea what to do with a stray... I was barely taking care of myself! But she was so beautiful. I was just drawn to her."

"Yeah, I did NOT take you for being a cat person," Cristina teased.

"I wasn't," Lola responded, her voice low, holding eye contact with Jade. "But, like I said, it was a strange feeling, being drawn to protect her. Once I got her home and fed, it felt like she'd always been there." Lola let out a huff through her nose. "Honestly, Jade and I have had a strange relationship right from the beginning. I mean, everything was normal, but... well, you won't believe me," she chuckled, breaking the stare with Jade, her voice trembling slightly.

"No, say it, what?" Andrea managed to ask while stuffing another olive and cheese curd in her mouth.

Lola looked Andrea dead in the eyes, holding her gaze, and whispered, "I swear my cat has supernatural, almost psychic abilities. She can communicate with me, and I with her. I have freaking conversations with her," Lola exclaimed, her voice having risen with every word. Now she felt a flush of embarrassment, but she also felt so relieved to tell someone other than Jax. She took a gulp of tea and exhaled in relief.

The group stared at each other in disbelief, exchanging glances of worry, confusion, and uncertainty. Lucy, the jester of the bunch, exploded into laughter, breaking the awkward silence. "No way! Impossible! You've gone crazy. How did you even discover that?" As she laughed, she took a piece of chocolate pound cake Andrea had made herself, obviously not expecting Lola to respond.

Lola smoothed her skirt and shrugged, "It was a coincidence, it just happened. One day, I was at home watching TV and heard this voice in my head--'How boring, change the channel.' "

Lucy stopped chewing and stared incredulously at Lola, then at Jade, and back to Lola.

"And it turned out to be my cat, who was sitting on the sofa next to me," Lola continued, nonchalantly taking a piece of cake for herself. She paused for a moment while they all processed what she had said, then went on, "At first I thought I was going crazy. I mean, who hears voices in their head?" she mumbled with a mouthful of cake. "But then after several episodes like that I realized it was real. So I started talking to her mentally," Lola gestured with her free hand, pointing at her head, "and she replied back." As Lola nervously shared, she wiped her hands aimlessly on her skirt, grabbed her crochet project that was in the wicker basket next to her against the wall and started nervously crocheting the sweater she was making for Jax. It was the perfect distraction to keep her hands busy, and avoid the curious stares of her friends.

Andrea let out a nervous laugh as she leaned forward, "Oh my gosh, were you freaked out?! What did you do?" she questioned, clearly amused but unsure if she believed it or not.

"Yeah," Cristina encouraged with an incredulous smile, "tell us!"

"Well," Lola continued slowly, her face lighting up as if recalling a fond memory, "she tells me everything from what she likes to do, to what she thinks of people. It's very fun..."

The three girls hung on her every word, eyes wide with fascination and skepticism. The group moved closer around the table in the living room, sipping on their teas and specialty coffee Lucy had brought over. The flickering flames of the gas fireplace cast a warm glow across their faces as they waited for Lola to recount more stories about Jade, though most of them were still not fully convinced.

"Okay, how about this, the other day she told me to buy her some tuna cans because the ones she had were expired. And I told her it couldn't be because I had *just* bought them recently. And she said, 'Check the date.' And it turned out the little hairball was right! The cans had been expired for two months." Lola giggled, taking a sip of her coffee.

Jade sneezed and settled into the all-paws-tucked-in position, giving them slow, sleepy blinks. Lola could tell she liked being talked about. "Your cat is so smart!" Lucy exclaimed, taking her blonde hair in her hands and twirling the ends over her shoulder.

"Yes, she's very smart." Lola replied proudly, and continued working on the sweater.

I am, Jade whispers sleepily.

"Doesn't it bother you? Her just being in your head, hearing her voice?" Andrea asked, her dark eyes scrutinizing.

"No, not at all. I love it. She keeps me company. I was very lonely in the city," Lola confessed, pausing in her work. "She also gives me very useful advice," Lola smiled, happy to change the subject.

Andrea looked intrigued, "What kind of advice?"

"Well, advice about my love life, for example. She tells me who I should date and who I shouldn't." A blush appeared on Lola's cheeks.

"Oh, come on! And how does your cat know that?" Lucy teased, spilling some of her coffee, when she leaned back giggling.

Lola grabbed a napkin and wiped up her friend's spilled coffee as she answered. "Well, because she has a sixth sense for these things. She knows who's good for me and who's not," she confirmed in a matter of fact manner.

"And what has she told you so far?" Cristina asked with genuine interest, pouring Lucy some more coffee.

"Well, she's told me to avoid Marco, a detective who came to the shop this morning. I guess he's here because of the taxi driver's murder."

"Why did she tell you that?" Andrea wondered.

"Well, because she says that Marco, um, smells bad," Lola replied. She shrugged her shoulders, eyeing Jade who was completely ignoring Lola and quite possibly snoring.

They all burst into laughter at the absurdity of it.

"That's hilarious!" Cristina exclaimed, still chuckling. She pushed her plate away and leaned back before wiping her mouth with a napkin and reapplying her lip-gloss.

"Yeah," Lola continued with a sigh, "and the worst part is, I actually think he's kinda cute. His eyes, oh my, and his accent..." she blushed, hiding her head in her orange yarn.

"Well, I think you should give him a chance. Maybe your cat is wrong. She's not infallible, right?" Lucy suggested, as she glanced at Jade.

"Maybe..." Lola trailed off, her thoughts consumed by the idea of the handsome detective...and Jade's warning.

You're simplifying my expert advice in a very human way, Jade said indignantly, sharing her thoughts for the first time that night.

No, I'm saying exactly what you said, Lola answered.

What about the subtlety of the smells I mentioned? Is it the same for you to smell something bad as it is for me to smell something bad? Jade opened her eyes, questioning Lola.

Well... yes, no.. wait, I don't know! Lola huffed.

Cristina stared at Lola, wondering what was wrong. Andrea and Lucy noticed too. All three of them turned and looked at Jade.

The human language has too many limitations. Can we communicate with meows? I think you could understand me better, Jade replied with annoyance, blinking slowly once again.

"Meow!" Lola screeched loudly, startling all her friends. There wasn't one who didn't wonder about her friend's sanity.

Did I say something? Lola asked, resuming her crocheting, oblivious to her human friends' reactions.

Rotten potatoes.

Lola paused, looking up excitedly. *Really?*

No. You don't know how to meow. Jade closed her eyes completely.

"What. Was. That, Lola?" Cristina asked, laughing nervously and looking thoroughly freaked out.

"Oh, sorry, Cris, Jade asked me to meow," Lola replied, very seriously, looking at her crocheted sleeve to fix a stitch.

All the girls looked at each other. For a second, Lola thought she saw Lucy's gaze directed towards the door when she glanced up.

"I don't, I don't understand, are you communicating with Jade right now?" Andrea asked with genuine curiosity, moving onto her knees, leaning forward.

"Yes..." Lola hesitated, slightly. She realized, this just got real.

"Hey, don't want to sound like I don't believe you. I mean, I do, I do," Andrea fidgeted, "I do, but... could you give us a demonstration?"

Lola smiled, "Hey, I get it, this is a hefty dose of weird. I don't blame you. So, sure, yeah...why not." She put down her crocheting and faced the girls and Jade.

Jade, if you don't want to eat the typical cat food for the next week, you better help me with this, Lola pressed.

Jade opened her eyes wide.

"We'll do a demonstration," Lola said confidently.

"Yeah!" Andrea exclaimed, clapping with delight. The other two quickly joined her, intrigued by the whole situation, lightening the mood. "Okay, you say she's like psychic or something, right? Then Jade," Andrea asked, turning to face the cat that was now sitting up, staring intently at the one who called her, "what did I have to eat today?"

After a moment, Jade sneezed, and quickly used her paw to rub her nose. *Yuck! How can broccoli smell so bad? I've never smelled a human with such bad breath, this is an insult to me for lending myself to this stupid game and I hope you pay me back with tuna...*

"Broccoli," Lola said, with a firm and determined voice that broke through the silence in the room. All the girls looked at Andrea with their eyes wide open, as if they were shocked by the realization of what just happened. She slowly nodded her head in surprise and awe, biting her lip lightly as she stared at Lola, who was sitting tall and proud, a big goofy smile on her face.

"Okay, I will admit that was pretty impressive," said Cristina, freezing her smile. "Wait! Has Jade said anything to you about the murder? Might she understand something that humans don't?"

"Wait, wait, I don't really know much about this, what happened? I have seen that in the news and I've heard it mentioned literally everywhere, I just haven't paid much attention to it," Lucy asked confusedly.

Lola began explaining calmly but with a hint of mystery in her voice, "They found Daniel Smith in his house with a poisoned coffee cup and a haiku on his chest." She shifted her weight, turning more towards her friends and away from Jade, who started stretching, arching her back high and making her fur stand on end.

Lucy frowned in confusion, "A haiku? What's that?"

"It's a type of Japanese poem that has three lines and a total of seventeen syllables in a particular pattern," explained Lola, picking up her crochet needle, waving her hands gracefully like she was writing out the haiku in the air.

Andrea leaned forward with curiosity in her eyes as she asked, "What did the poem say?"

Lola took a long pause before meeting her gaze and reciting,

"The withered flower,
deceiving of one's own self,
justice blooms for them".

Cristina gasped in shock while covering her mouth with one hand. "I can't believe this is happening here in Jaramillo." She whispered, getting closer to Lola. "What does it mean?"

Lola shrugged her shoulders before replying, "Heck if I know. No one does - at least no one has come forward. It's still a mystery. It has to be why a detective is in town."

Lola looked over at Jade who had moved to the black loveseat and was sleeping after the broccoli test. Jade opened an eye and thought to Lola: *Don't bother me. I'm dreaming about mice.*

Lola smiled and responded, *Come on, Jade. Be a good girl and help us with the case. You're the expert in poetry.*

Jade opened her other eye, yawned long and big, showing her razor-sharp teeth, slowly blinked and replied, *I'm not an expert in poetry. I'm an expert in catching mice. And taking naps...I only happen to like poetry. Now, leave me be - death, broccoli, and burnt wood smells have made me irritable.*

"She says she's not an expert in poetry... Someone will have less tuna this week," Lola promised with a snicker.

"Is she usually this stubborn?" Andrea asked, crossing her arms, no longer impressed. "But then again," Andrea uncrossed her arms and sat up straighter, "I remember that article, but...there was no mention of the coffee being poisoned."

Lola shook her head, not wanting to believe what she was hearing. "No, it had to have mentioned it, else how would I know?" she said, looking over at Andrea, puzzled.

"There's no other explanation," Andrea replied matter-of-factly. "except..." turning her head towards a sleeping Jade, pausing for a moment, thinking about the implications of it all before finally saying, "it's absolutely chilling that Jade could've told you this and you didn't even realize," her voice somber and serious.

Lucy nodded in agreement, eyeing both Jade and Lola. Cristina, trying not to look as bothered, busied herself with pouring another cup of coffee. "I would've been all over that coffee brand if the news gave away *that* tidbit," Lucy straightened up, now that she had the floor, "after all, I have to do my due diligence and make sure it's not a nation-wide poisoning. I serve premium coffees every day at my boutique, *Shea-Café.* There's no way he could've gotten it from me and then been killed by it, right?. Na-uh, no way."

Cristina tipped her head. "Well, now that you mention it Lucy...isn't he the cabby that always bad-mouthed your café when he would pick up tourists? I mean, there was that one time, he picked up an Instagram influencer, with like, a million followers, and she totally did a Live video right outside the café and went on and on about, 'this café here is a total rip-off. The coffees, my cabby says, aren't even international, so you should get your coffee somewhere else' – so maybe..."

Lucy thought for a moment before her eyes narrowed with realization, interrupting her. "Oh my god!"

"Oh yeah, I saw that! I follow her and was hoping to get a selfie once I saw she was on the island," Andrea said nonchalantly, unaware that her friend was upset.

"No, no, now that I think about it, I ran into Sophia, you know, the tour guide lady, Lola," Cristina chimed in, having put her coffee down, no longer interested in drinking it, "at the café and she had actually just finished having coffee with a long-time friend, I forget her name, anyway, she was saying how the cabby was all nervous and anxious that day, he missed her turn two times! She was starting to freak out when he finally just dropped her off at the travel agent's office. Apparently, Sophia remembered it so vividly because she called Daniel to find out what was wrong - I mean, he's literally like the *only* cabby on the island for all these tourists."

"So, what was his problem?" Lola leaned in, thankful the conversation steered away from her.

"She never did find out. She called him several times but he never answered. I think that was the day after you arrived, Lola."

An uncomfortable silence permeated the room, making the air feel heavy while the soft amber flames radiated strange shadows in the room. Everything paused and tension hung in the air. Suspicious eyes settled on Lola, but she was staring at the floor.

She took a breath, "I don't know how I know about the coffee," Lola whispered, "but I was with Jax - I was moving in." Lola finally looked up, her hands, slightly trembling, thinking her friends might actually suspect *her*.

Jade starts yakking up a sticky, white-ish, gelatinous hairball. *Oh my god, how embarrassing. Lola, calm down, my stomach is in knots!*

"That's nasty," Lucy grimaced. Cristina made a gagging sound and turned away. Andrea covered her mouth, instantly turning her head away, squeezing her eyes shut.

Lola, relieved for the distraction, immediately shot up, "Oh, Jade, you poor thing."

"Seriously, Lola, that's gross, can you please clean it up, I'm about to hurl my chocolate cake," Andrea mumbled through her fingers, still covering her mouth, as if the force of vomit would be held back by her dainty fingers.

"Ugh, I got it. I have cats, I know the drill," Lucy pushed herself off the floor with a grunt and headed toward the kitchen in search of paper towels.

Lola scooped Jade into her arms and started consoling her, which in turn, calmed herself. Lola cradled her like an infant, rubbing her belly in a clockwise motion; Jade completely surrendered in her arms, thankful for the attention after the unexpected gastrointestinal disruption.

Staring out the window, framed in the moonlight, Lola calmed both of their nerves with the affectionate strokes. She took a long, deep breath and faced her friends.

Lucy finished cleaning the goopy mess, virtually unphased while Andrea took sips of tea, her elbows resting on the table, and Cristina, snacking on cake once again, briefly paused when she met Lola's eyes. "Thanks, I don't know what came over her," Lola sat down on the black couch, opposite of the loveseat Andrea was now sitting in, her legs folded under her. Jade reoriented herself in her lap, purring softly, blinking slowly at the suspecting friends.

"Well, I think it's just crazy that you were probably the last person to see Daniel alive," Cristina quipped.

"Yeah, pretty weird, but Lucy, you could've totally done it!" Andrea roared, pointing her well-manicured silver nails at her, "he totally bashed your café...probably only because his ex *loves* the coffee there."

Lucy, hurled a half done crochet doll that she had grabbed from Lola's crochet basket right at Andrea's head. Andrea easily dodged the attack, laughing hysterically.

"Hey, you all, that isn't funny! Someone could be a suspect here," Lola said, trying to make her face serious and her eyes stern. Jade meowed her displeasure at the sudden outburst, but quickly forgave the women since they had ceased making Lola feel anxious. She did not like it when these humans made her upset. "Seriously, though," Lola continued, catching her breath, "I think we need to take this seriously and figure out what happened. Remember, I had an unexpected visitor today at the shop."

The girls' laughter died down as they watched Lola's expression turn serious. "What kind of visitor?" Lucy asked.

"The detective I mentioned earlier. Posing as a customer no less."

"So, he tried to trick you?" There was an accusatory tone in Cristina's voice; she had no time for men who played games.

"Yes, no, well, I don't know. He didn't say he was a detective, Jade actually did." Lola looked down at her companion, who squirmed onto her back for an obvious belly rub. "Jade read the name on his briefcase as I was showing him some of our historical literature and told me."

"Whoa," Cristina whispered in awe.

"That's why I need Jade, to find out who the killer is before they think it was me."

After another uncomfortable moment of silence, Cristina burst out, "Of course it wasn't!" breaking the tension, chuckling nervously.

"I definitely think you're one of the most harmless beings in the world," Lucy affirmed.

The friends immediately tried to change the subject, staring at what was left of the food, but Lola's phone lit up with a stunted buzz. She had received a text.

Wiggling the phone out of her skirt pocket under a limp Jade, she saw it was from her employee, Charles, before the screen went dark. She toggled the phone on with one hand and opened up her Messages. The message was brief and made her heart skip a beat:

"Brandon's father has been found dead. Brandon has been arrested. He won't be at work tomorrow, I guess I'll take his shift."

4

— ◆ —

CHAPTER 4

"*I* always believed I deserved more. Perhaps that was my mistake, the reason for my corruption. But it's impossible to escape it when it's been inside you, when it's constantly your best friend's soulmate. I hope this makes up for my sorrow." The Killer.

Jaramillo in the summer was a bright and cheerful place, full of sun and tourists. This week, however, was dark and miserable, full of clouds and mystery. The weather reflected the moods of the locals. The death of Randall was all anyone could talk about. Especially when the local newspaper published the haiku that had been left on the corpse.

"A poor orphaned soul,

deprived of love and guidance.

Guilt eats him alive."

It had only been a few days since the latest murder in this cozy town but life went on, the tourists kept coming, and Lola had to continue running her antique shop as if nothing had happened. After the eventful night with her girlfriends, Jade has been sticking to Lola like white on rice ever since she felt Lola's anxiousness, which has never happened before. Jade was like a hovering helicopter mother! Thank goodness she didn't have a boyfriend.

The chimes above the door sounded. "I'll be right with you," Lola shouted, as she finished arranging the latest addition in a glass case: a bronze statue by Albert-ernest Carrier-belleuse titled "La Mélodie". Lola stood after locking the sliding door and let out a small gasp.

"What brings you here, Detective?" she asked, as she noticed he was dressed more casually in slim khaki jogger pants and a V-neck black t-shirt. She knew that the presence of a detective, no matter how attractive, was not a good sign. Jade appeared next to Lola with a silent leap from behind the counter. The detective hesitated for a moment seeing her appear so suddenly. She sat down, unblinking, swishing her tail back and forth across the glass top.

"I stopped by to ask you some questions," the Detective announced, closing the distance between him and Lola, moving slightly to the side away from the unnerving cat.

"What kind of questions? I don't know how I can help you, Detective."

"Please, call me Marco."

"Marco," Lola echoed, slightly blushing.

Jade hissed.

"Sorry," Lola gasped, grabbing her cat before she could cause any more trouble. "Jade doesn't like strangers."

Wait, wait, no, I'll be good, promise... even in front of Detective horse face!

Marco smiled, brushing off the incident as if it were nothing. He pulled out a notebook and pen, not skipping a beat with Jade's interjection.

"There," Lola sighed, closing the back door with Jade protesting loudly behind it. Turning back to Marco, she gestured toward the charming dining set from the early 1900s in a striking Jacobean style. "Please, have a seat. May I get you some tea?"

"No, thank you," Marco politely declined, taking a seat closest to the wall next to the window overlooking the front of the shop.

Lola grabbed her cup of tea from behind the counter, flipped the "OPEN" sign on the door to "CLOSED", and sat opposite the detective.

She took a sip of tea, and settled back in the ornate chair before speaking, "What did you want to ask me?"

Jade continued meowing loudly from behind the door. The hair on the back of Lola's neck stood up, and she began to take short shallow breaths as she felt Jade's distress.

Marco continued speaking, saying something about how both she and Brandon were considered suspects, but Lola wasn't listening. She was stuck in between being present with Marco and Jade's incessant need to be released; she wasn't able to block what was happening.

"Lola!"

"Wha-what?!" Lola startled, finally snapping out of the trance.

"Where were you? It's like you were staring right through me," Marco said, putting down his pen, seeming to be genuinely concerned about Lola. The color had drained from her face, making her emerald-green eyes a stark contrast to her pale olive skin-tone. Marco gently continued, "It's alarming to see you so pale and out of it."

"I'm sorry, I'm just so upset about these murders," Lola deflected as she took a sip of tea.

Jade stopped making noise.

"The department has reason to suspect that the poison used in a murder came from your shop," he started again, seeing some color return to Lola's face. "We had one person of interest, but isn't any longer since, we, uh," Marco hesitated to continue, but after making eye contact with Lola's eyes again, he seemed to make the decision to be honest. "Well, Richard, the man we first suspected, was seen at home at the time of Randall's murder, which rules him out."

"Which leaves Brandon, Charles...or me," Lola shuddered, meeting Marco's eyes for a brief moment before looking back down at her empty cup.

The chimes over the door rang and a voice exploded in Lola's head. *Don't ever do that again!*

"Holy...Shhhhh!" cried Marco, his legs striking the rim of the table as he tumbled back against the wall, almost knocking it over. Lola thought he was going to break the $4000 table over a cat!

"Jade! Really?" Lola was not a bit surprised, steadying the table. "Sorry, she can, uh, wiggle and jiggle the handle," Lola explained, motioning with her hand. Jade, unfazed by Marco's sudden reaction, leapt up and took her regular place in the sill of the bay window next to them. She casually licked her paw, paused, with her tongue between her teeth, and eyed Marco who was still looking incredulously at her.

Clearing his throat, appearing slightly embarrassed over a cat startling him, Marco, pulled his chair away from the wall and sat back down. Lola lowered her head so Marco wouldn't see the small smile spreading across her lips. *Who would've thought a detective like him could be so jumpy?* She side-eyed Jade who was now washing her face with her paw.

While he said that Richard had largely been ruled out because he was under surveillance when Randall theoretically died, Marco's tone made him sound unconvinced. Brandon had clear motives: he had recently fought with his father, Randall, in front of everyone, and it was known that their relationship was difficult. Lola pondered to herself, watching Marco scribble something on the pad.

"There are a couple coincidences here, Lola," Marco said, looking up from his pad. "You were the last one to see both victims, and this poem, the haiku. You're familiar with poetry, yes?" Marco paused, watching Lola's reaction. She didn't flinch, her eyes, fixated on him, narrowed in thought, no glassy stare this time.

"Yes, my writing specialty is free verse poetry," Lola confirmed, almost instantly regretting she had said that.

Marco tapped the end of the pen on his pad, stopped, looked at his notes then back at her, "You got into town just before the first murder, correct?"

"That's what everyone is saying," Lola chuckled nervously, tucking a strand of hair behind her ear, glancing away from his intense gaze.

Lola understood the seriousness of coincidences: she was now an official suspect.

***

The morning progressed as usual: a customer came in, asked questions, and left. Another customer came in, got excited about a product, saw the price, and left. Yet another customer came in, made a purchase, chatted for a while, and left. Someone offered them a "great deal" which turned out to be a worthless antique. Another person offered them a product without knowing if it had any value.

However, Lola's mind wasn't on antiquities. *"You got into town just before the first murder, correct?"* Marco's voice kept echoing in her head. Ever since Detective Marco abruptly left after receiving a phone call, Lola wasn't feeling very secure lately. Talk about inconvenient coincidences, Lola thought.

Lola thanked the latest customer for coming in, even though the lamp was worthless, she wanted a reason to catalog it in the back room.

A cool $20 was worth it. A quick bribe and smile convinced Charles to cover the rest of the afternoon; Lola had to think.

A few moments later, lounging on her couch, Lola was feeling desperate. She looked again at the haikus, printed so boldly in the paper with no resolution. Lola ran her hand through her auburn-streaked hair as she sighed softly and muttered to herself, "I don't know. It's all so confusing." She noticed Jade sleeping peacefully on the couch. "I wonder if my tuna-loving fur baby wants to help me?" Lola said, looking slyly at Jade with determination in her deep green eyes.

The cat stirred a bit and opened an eye, her green eyes speckled with gold and met Lola's gaze. Jade replied sleepily to Lola, *Don't bother me. I was dreaming of a plate of tuna, which by the way you owe me, traitor, villain, rogue, bandit. You still haven't bought tuna, have you?*

Lola ignored her and pleaded, *I need your input for this, Jade. What clue could be in this haiku?* Lola shook the newspaper toward Jade pointing at the headline, which read in big bold black letters: **DEATH STRIKES AGAIN WITH ANOTHER DEADLY POEM.** *See, right here, they took another snapshot of it. Look! It's clearly about Brandon, but... What could it have to do with Daniel and his scandal with Richard?*

Biting her nail slightly, Lola recited out loud,

"A poor orphaned soul,

deprived of love and guidance.

Guilt eats him alive."

Still upset about not having tuna, Jade yawned widely and stretched before saying *I'll check it out after my nap. Let me sleep. I engaged in a trial of strength with a large, hairy feline last night and I'm exhausted."* The cat curled up again, shifting a bit on the couch, and settled back into the land of dreams.

Rolling her head back, Lola closed her eyes, dropped the newspaper on the coffee table and slumped back onto the couch. She closed her eyes, placing one arm over her head scratching - trying to think of a solution. "Oh!" Lola exclaimed, face palming her forehead.

Jax is a writer, duh, maybe he can help me!

Jade's eyes opened wide, she sprang up, rising on all fours, arching her back, instantly awake from her nap. She looked at Lola with disdain and started to meow.

Jax? That guy is a disaster at writing. Jade paused and let out a small disapproving purr before continuing. *I read one of his books, and it was so bad that I used it for my litter box."*

Lola was puzzled. *What kind of writer is Jax now? I haven't read anything from him in a while.*

Jade's tail twitched as she considered her response. *Well, in my humble feline opinion, he's a pretty mediocre writer,* she meowed with an air of superiority. Her white whiskers twitched, accentuating her puffed-up fur and disdainful kitty-cat expression. *"He writes in a monotone manner, lacking the excitement that a natural hunter, like me, wants to feel."*

Lola couldn't help but laugh at her cat's arrogant stance. *"And what about his poetry?"* Lola asked, curious to know more.

Jade recoiled and began to meow with disdain, *Oh, his poetry! It's like he's trying to be a cat, but without the grace or elegance. It's like he's writing about mice without ever having hunted them in his life.* She dramatically swished her tail back and forth as she spoke, ending with an almost disgusted expression on her feline face. *If Marco is a horse, Jax is a seal out of water.*

Lola, who was drinking her coffee, had to make a tremendous effort not to spit it all out. *Well, not everyone can be expert yet graceful hunters and like you, Jade,"* Lola joked.

Jade looked at her with narrowed eyes and hissed before continuing. *Of course not,* Jade responded with a meow. *Only those who have the necessary skill and instinct can be as skilled at hunting as I am. Jax, on the other hand, should find something else to do. Like crochet.*

Jade got off the couch with a satisfied stretch and Lola, ignoring her insult, glanced around the room, absentmindedly pulling out some leftover ham from her lunch container that was on the glass table in front of her. Her gaze settled onto the window, and she couldn't help but focus on the world outside.

Lola gave her some of the cooked ham she wasn't going to eat and stroked her ear as Jade gently gobbled up the piece of food. "Well, maybe he's not the best writer in the world, but I need his help," Lola said.

Jade rolled her cat eyes like none other and yawned before speaking again. *Suit yourself,* Jade resigned, as she licked her paw. *But if you bother me during my nap again, I swear I'll bite your toes. By the way, they've been smelling a bit lately...get a pedicure.*

Lola looked at Jade with narrowed eyes, but she was already looking for the perfect nap spot.

Good luck with Jax, Jade said, distracted.

Lola smiled and stroked her cat's head.

*I might catch a bird...*Jade yawned again. *Maybe in a few hours.*

Jade closed her eyes and lay down on a part of the floor where the sun filtering through the window was warming, while Lola left the house in search of Jax, the only other person who understands the value of words - even if they are deadly.

5

— · —

CHAPTER 5

About ready to head out the back door of the shop, Lola instead found her brother in the antique store office. She was relieved he was right where she needed him the most.

The sun was setting as Lola and Jax entered the back storage room of the store, where an antique mirror was leaning against the wall. Its dark frame seemed to swallow up the remaining light, and Lola felt a chill run down her spine. Lately, she had been very jumpy. As she glanced at herself briefly before catching her twin's matching pair of emerald eyes, she wasn't sure if this was something she could handle.

"Tell me the haiku again, Sis, I want to hear it," Jax said with a slight smile, putting her back at ease. She found herself starting to like Japanese poems.

Next thing the twins realized, almost forty minutes had passed and they had found nothing new while studying the haiku line by line. Another ten minutes passed, and Jax thought he had found a clue in the initials of the haikus, displayed within the news article, but no, he was wrong. By the time an hour had passed, they both gave up. The night had already invaded Jaramillo, they were exhausted, and there were still things to do before closing time.

"I really can't find any clues in the haikus," Jax said with a sigh as he tossed the national newspaper where he had been reading them, rubbing his brow. The case had gained national attention by this time, and each of those Japanese poems were plastered all over the front page. Experts from different fields tried to extract clues from them: psychologists, writers, graphologists, and other professionals analyzed the haikus to no avail.

"Me neither," Lola replied, leaning on the wobbly table that she shared with her brother in the secluded area of the antique store before letting herself flop back onto an enormous 1950s armchair.

"But I was thinking about something..." Jax said hesitantly. His eyes searched for his sister's as he rubbed his hands together.

"What?" Lola asked curiously, lethargy leaving her body.

No matter what happened, there was always a link back to Lola and it was only a matter of time before national media picked up on her name; Jax wasn't going to let that happen.

Lola sat up straight and then leaned forward, resting her elbows on her knees and her chin in her palms with her eyes fixed on her brother.

"One of the clients at the salon I'll have tomorrow was a teacher at Brandon's school. I bet I can-"

"Jax! Crocodiles and chocolates! JAX!" Charles shouted from the counter of the store.

"What's going on? Why are you yelling?" Jax shouted back, storming towards the front of the store with Lola right at his heels. Jax wasn't too fond of Charles to begin with, and he didn't bother to hide his annoyance once he got to the counter where Charles was half sneering, half smiling. It was an odd sight to say the least.

"Oh, I'm yelling because sometimes I feel like yelling about the crocodiles we don't have and the chocolate I *do* want to have!" Charles said, chuckling at his own bad joke. There was a break in his voice that belied his frustration about something. He ran his hand over his face, settling just under his chin, looking down at Jax who was about a head shorter than he.

"Wha...what happened?" Jax asked, leaning on the counter and looking around, searching for a reason for Charles' frustration.

"A lot of things happened in the world, today, son: tsunamis, earthquakes, wars, ...me forgetting to tell you that the 1930 English pocket watch you sold today was already on hold for a customer. Then there's famines, plagues..." Charles said all in one breath, tapping his foot nervously on the floor while looking at a deposit slip made out to "Annie".

Lola noticed the watch's description and an exorbitant price listed next to it as the final price of the watch. She stood there, remembering faintly about a customer interested in that particular watch.

"Wait... What?" Jax said, confused. "You forgot to tell me the watch was on hold?" Jax's irritation was growing by the second. First, zero clues and now an employee who seemingly can't remember to set aside a stupid watch?

"Well, I think you've understood the problem," Charles replied, waving the customer's receipt in front of him, "and now I have to fix it."

Lola, who had been listening to the whole problem, decided to stay out of it; if they couldn't fix it by tomorrow, she would find a way. She quietly made her way over to the antique table set where she had sat with Marco a few days ago. She decided to take out the sweater she was knitting for Jax from her bag that she had brought down with her that morning in case the store was having a slow day.

Settling into one of the armchairs closest to the store's entrance, she was now working on the other sleeve, certain she wouldn't make the same mistake she had earlier on the right side. It was a good way to stop thinking about murders and wait until closing time, though she was doubtful any customers would come in.

Jax grumbled something under his breath, exasperated, turned and started walking towards the door. "Let's go for a beer after work," he said, looking around at Lola and Charles. "We can figure this out tomorrow."

Lola looked up from her crocheting and smiled, putting it in her bag before standing up. She was looking forward to getting out of the store, taking a load off after a long day of work. The trio closed the business early with Charles locking the door and silently following Jax as they stepped out into the evening air - what could go wrong with a beer?

***

They made their way down the street until they reached their favorite bar - The Poet's Corner. The bar was only a few blocks away, so they decided to go for an island stroll instead of catching a cab. The streets were quite empty as it was past peak hours so there wasn't much traffic; just an occasional car passing by every now and then. The sky was full of stars but obscured by clouds drifting lazily across, making their night look quite gloomy yet peaceful.

"Another busy night!" Jax exclaimed sarcastically after he spotted an empty booth near one of the walls. He motioned for the others to follow him as he jogged over to claim it before anyone else did.

Charles laughed, shaking his head at Jax's enthusiasm. "You never change," he said with a smile on his face and followed Lola, who was taking a seat next to Jax in the booth. They placed their drink orders with the online bar app and within a few minutes a server appeared carrying all three beverages: beer for Charles and Lola and whisky neat for Jax.

"So, tell me," Jax said as he lifted his glass of whiskey to his lips, "what happened with that watch? How did you forget about that?"

Charles sighed heavily before taking a sip from his own drink. "Well," he began, "I forgot to tell you about Annie's hold on it because I'm pulling a double with Brandon in jail." He nodded sadly before continuing on, "There's not much of anything else to say really. I'm going to have to figure out how to make this right."

At that moment, a man approached the table. He wore a black baseball hat and an old chestnut leather jacket. He slightly nodded his head at Lola before settling in the booth next to Charles. A smile appeared on his lips as he leaned forward, gazing at Lola with what seemed like admiration in his deep set eyes. "What a surprise to find you here, Lola," he said, turning to Charles, nodding. "What's got you guys looking so serious?"

Lola looked at Marco, blushing with embarrassment before quickly diverting her gaze to her beer bottle. She couldn't help but think she must look like a mess after the long day! Jax frowned and Charles tried not to laugh; it was clear that neither of them had expected him.

"Ah, nothing important," said Jax, waving it off. "We were just discussing some business matters."

Marco smiled broadly at Jax's response before leaning back in his seat with a sigh of satisfaction; although it seemed like there were still more questions he wanted to ask, dancing on the tip of his tongue. "Tell me," he said, directing his gaze at Lola. "When is a good time to finish our conversation? I still have more questions about the last two victims."

Charles and Jax exchanged a concerned look as Lola's body flushed with nervousness. "I don't know," she replied softly, her gaze fixed on the bottle in her hands.

Marco laughed and raised his glass. "I am officially off-duty, so no more crime-talk; I need a break," he proclaimed before taking another sip of his beer. He reached out towards the trio, waiting for a toast. The three obliged and the clinking of glasses was the first of many.

Two hours later, with no talk about murder and a lot of laughter, it felt like a night on a vacation island with friends. Marco suddenly extended his hand to Lola with a mischievous twinkle in his eyes. She wondered if he would be like this if he hadn't had a little to drink.

"You're the private investigator, right? The one on Brandon's murder case..." Charles interrupted Lola's thoughts, slapping the detective's hand as if he was giving him a high-five.

"Yes, I am," replied Marco, clearing his throat, retreating his hand back to his glass.

"Brandon is my friend... or ...something like that. He's incapable of killing anyone. You know that, right?" said Charles, with a hint of pleading at the end.

"I'm not here to discuss the case, buddy. I'm sorry. In fact, I came here to get away from the case," he said, sounding cheerful, taking another long drag of his beer. Marco breathed, setting the empty bottle on the table, sitting back even further against the booth and asked, "What else is there about this town I don't know about, yet?"

As they spread nonsensical rumors amongst each other, the mood lightened as they became more comfortable around each other, alcohol surely playing a helping role. "And the girlfriend- the girlfriend put laxatives in his coffee!" Charles sputtered, laughing until tears streamed down his face. "He had to run home for obvious reasons."

Everyone roared with laughter, Marco seeming especially amused. On his turn, he told a rumor about an old man who had been coming home smelling of a woman's perfume - the wife thought he was cheating. "Turns out, "Marco slurred, trying to keep his composure, "he genuinely thought he was putting on men's cologne to impress her so she'd want to... *get busy*," Marco waggled his eyebrows and elbowed Charles in the ribs with a wink.

Charles doubled over, nearly hyperventilating in laughter. Jax rolled his eyes, smiling, taking another sip of whiskey.

"And what about you? Do you sometimes go home with a woman's perfume on you?" asked Lola, with inquisitive eyes.

"That's a very private question for a private detective, miss," replied Marco, winking at her. "By the way, what brand of perfume do you wear?" he joked. Lola gawked, but before she could answer, he got up abruptly, looked at his watch and announced, "I'm sorry to cut our pleasantries and juicy rumors short, but I must be going. I have an early morning meeting with a police officer."

The investigator bid farewell to the group, exhibiting no signs of his slight drunkenness, and disappeared into the crowd that had grown since they arrived.

A few minutes later, the three of them decided to call it a night as well.

"Lola, just a reminder that I don't work in the morning. My shift starts at noon. You remember that, right?" Charles asked as they pooled their money to pay for the drinks.

"Yes, I remember," she lied.

"And I'm going to sleep in tomorrow morning, sister. There's not much to do in the shop and I have to go to work in the afternoon at the saloon," Jax shrugged. Lola scowled at him. Her brother was only looking for an excuse not to help her. He returned her scowl with his best innocent look.

'Ugh, fine. You two are the worst employees."

The two men escorted Lola home and then headed to their own places. She said goodbye absentmindedly, her thoughts muddled and cloudy and troubled.

What if Marco was investigating them the whole time?

6

—·—

CHAPTER 6

The morning after, Lola's head was still fuzzy from a hangover and lost in her experience with the detective as she habitually got dressed for work. She had gone down from her house to the store to open it and had forgotten the key to the front door. She went back up the winding staircase, feeling a little woozy, grabbed the keys from the basket on the weathered oak table stand next to the front door, went back down to open it, and realized she had forgotten her phone. *If a hangover is going to cause me to work out this much, I should go to the bar more often.*

When she went down for the third time, she could only laugh when she realized she had forgotten the sweater she was crocheting for Jax. She felt completely scatterbrained and was grateful that she was alone in the shop that day and not responsible for directing anyone else. She craved a little solitude after last night. There wouldn't be much to do at the antique store that morning besides attending to customers; there were no new products to analyze, nor any maintenance work to do.

Lola opened the door to the store and flipped the sign from CLOSED to OPEN. She took a minute to appreciate the morning ocean breeze, truly feeling like home again. That day, the sun seemed to want to shine brighter than usual. Lola was really in a good mood, and even spilling the coffee she had brought from the back office didn't change the happiness that last night had brought.

Setting her coffee down, steam rising lazily into the streams of gold from the rising sun piercing through the windows, she sat to crochet a little. Customers didn't usually arrive so early, so she would have some peace and quiet for a while. Even though Lola does adore Charles and Jax, they can be very noisy in the morning. Jade is still off on her morning excursions, the silly cat. She had adjusted to island life quickly - she hated the city. That left Lola to enjoy a bit of solitude.

She had just gotten into the rhythm of her stitching when an all too familiar chime followed by footsteps interrupted her bliss.

It was Marco.

"Hello, Miss Lola. Busy this morning?" Marco's voice was low, almost gruff and gravely like he'd been in a yelling match for hours on end.

Lola looked up from the sweater and scrutinized him with tired eyes. After a few moments of uncomfortable silence, she finally spoke. "Hi, Detective. Not exactly, what can I do for you? We don't serve alcohol here," she snickered playfully...even with a dull throbbing headache to remind her why she doesn't drink often.

"Well, actually I wanted to invite you for a walk around the city with me. There's a travel agency that offers guided tours and I thought it would be a good idea." He looked away, lowering his sunglasses, squinting as he took in the rest of the empty shop and hoping his offer wouldn't be seen as too intrusive.

"A walk? Why?" Her voice rose an octave, mixed with suspicion.

"Well, I have some questions for you about the haikus that the killer has left at the crime scenes. You told me you were a writer and I think maybe you could help me." His shoulders were stiff as he waited for her response, trying to look professional. His stomach gurgled...loudly. Lola's intense gaze seemed to make him even more uneasy.

Lola relented, took a sip of coffee with her free hand and sighed heavily. "I guess I can try. But I'm not an expert in Japanese poetry or anything like that, and I haven't found anything on my own, just so you know, " she quickly added. "But maybe working together we can prove that a coincidence is just that...*a coincidence.*"

Relief flooded Marco's face, and he gave her a grateful smile. "I want to help you prove it. That's why I want you to come with me to explore the city; besides, I'm new here," Marco added.

"Okay, I'll be available after noon, which is when Charles comes to work. Does that work for you?" Lola asked, twisting her hands a little and making a superhuman effort to maintain eye contact with the attractive detective, trying not to feel intimidated by him.

"Perfect. We'll meet in the main square downtown?" Marco asked, but it was more like a confirmation as he slid the sunglasses on. Ray Bans, Lola noticed. He turned around and left the store in one swift motion.

Lola watched him leave. He had a magnificent bearing, there's no denying that.

***

The hours passed in the antique store, and Lola found them to be extremely slow. Between there being few customers that day, and the expectation and anxiety generated by the tour with Marco, that morning was slow and thick. The alcohol from the night before was not exactly helpful.

When it was time and Charles relieved Lola, she bought a sandwich on the way to downtown Jaramillo, where she would meet Marco. It was a beautiful day, and a gentle breeze provided the perfect temperature for a tour around her childhood island home.

Marco was waiting for her in the main square along with a woman with kind blue eyes. Their guide, who introduced herself as Sophia, greeted her warmly. "Welcome! Are you ready to discover the charms of this beautiful city?"

"Yes," they both replied in unison, hiding their apprehensions under eager smiles.

"Perfect. Then please follow me."

Both followed the woman through the picturesque streets of Jaramillo. Lola couldn't help but marvel at the vibrant, sun-soaked downtown area as Marco remained stoic beside her. He was tall and strong, with a frame that seemed capable of shouldering any burden. His gaze drifted from building to building as if in search of something beyond what they could see.

She admired the buildings that surrounded the square, noting their different architectural styles as she followed behind the guide. So much has changed since she left the island.

"These buildings," began Sophia, gesturing at each one in turn with her outstretched arm, "are great examples of colonial-style architecture here in Jaramillo. Note how some have high ceilings and large windows while others have small archways and intricate stone carvings."

Marco walked down the street silently admiring its details as the guide explained their history. He lingered in front of a two-story structure with large balconies on either side and it seemed he had found what he was looking for. "What is this one?" Marco asked after a few moments of quiet contemplation.

"This is an old convent," responded Sophia, "built about three hundred years ago by Spanish missionaries who wanted to spread Christianity throughout the region. It's one of the oldest public buildings in Jaramillo."

Lola looked around with wide eyes and a sense of awe. She was captivated by the old building and its beautiful architecture, something she certainly didn't have respect for as a child. "It's so impressive!" she said, her voice filled with admiration.

Sophia smiled, obviously delighted to be able to share her knowledge with two interested tourists. She pointed at the intricately carved stone façade and explained how it was typical of the baroque style that had been popular in colonial times. She then went on to describe how each part of the building had its own special features; from the tall Doric columns supporting an imposing pediment, to the iron gates that protected the main entrance and even a large bell tower overlooking the convent grounds.

After a while, they had seen the main historic buildings and Sofia had spoken fondly about life in this small paradise. Marco hadn't talked much but when their eyes met, his gaze softened and she quickly glanced away, thankful for the sunglasses. She couldn't tell if her head was pounding because of the drinks or if her heart was truly flustered.

"Here we have one of the most beautiful squares in the town. As you can see, there's a fountain in the center and several benches and trees around. It's a very nice and peaceful place to walk and relax."

Lola stared out at the cobbled stones beneath her feet, her heart heavy with nostalgia. "Yes, it's very beautiful. I remember coming here to play with my friends when I was little," she said, looking at the fountain where cherished memories were made long ago.

"Ah, really? And what did you do around here?" Marco asked.

"Well, we would splash around in the fountain, climb the trees, eat ice cream from the corner shop..."

A glimmer of warmth shone through his brown eyes as he smiled faintly in response. "Sounds like fun," he replied.

"It was. We were very happy."

The two of them stood there together, basking in the beauty of the island's oldest, most majestic fountain until he unexpectedly broke the silence, "And what happened? Why did you leave town?"

She glanced up at him nervously before averting her gaze towards her hands. "Well, I wanted to be a writer," Lola answered quietly as if speaking it louder might give way to her failure. "And I thought I would have more opportunities to do that in the city on the mainland."

"And did you make it?" He pressed on, turning towards her with a genuine curiosity and concern that left her speechless for a moment.

"Not exactly," She replied after a moment. "I wrote some books, but none of them were successful. So, I did other jobs to survive."

He looked down at her with compassion in his eyes as though he understood all too well what it meant to try so hard only to end up empty handed yet again. "I'm sorry," He whispered softly in acknowledgement of all that she had been through.

"Don't worry." She said, waving her hand, "I don't regret trying. Plus, I'm back on the island now and I've inherited my aunt's antique business, you know. Maybe it's a sign that I need to start fresh," she sighed heavily, looking around toward the ocean; one could see from the square, with newfound hope.

"Of course, you will. I'm sure you'll do great with the business you've inherited," replied Marco, looking back at the fountain, tucking his hand in his jean pockets.

"Thank you, that's nice of you to say," Lola blushed.

"Sorry to interrupt, but we need to continue with the tour. Let's go see the church now, which is an architectural gem from the 18th century," said Sofia, shuffling them along across the way.

The trio entered the building, with Sofia leading the way. Lola stepped into the church, its hallowed walls reverberating with echoes of countless prayers. Bathed in sunlight from the stained glass windows, she felt a moment of reverent awe. He turned and looked at her, a faint smile on his lips as he closed the door behind them.

"Here we have the main altar," Sophia said as they approached it. Erected on the gilded marble dais was an ornate wooden statue of Saint Peter, patron saint of the city. Lola gazed in wonderment as rays of silvery and golden light illuminated the intricately carved details of his wooden effigy.

Next, Sophia led them inside the inner sanctum of the grandiose church, its infinite pillars reaching up to the entrenched dome. The air was thick with incense and all around them were statues of saints and martyrs standing with solemn faces against the backdrop of richly colored amber and midnight hued stained glass windows just at their backs. Rays of light shone through the stained glass of bronze, quartz, and blush-colored windows like divine beams, illuminating the altar at the far end of the church where the archangel, which had been lovingly crafted in gold and marble. Lola let out a gasp in wonderment at its beauty. She felt a presence next to her and noticed that Marco wasn't looking at the altar, but instead watching her.

"You told me your brother is a writer, right?" Marco whispered as Sophia talked in hushed tones, sharing more about the church. "Maybe he could help you interpret the haikus?"

"We've tried, but it hasn't worked," Lola interrupted with a hint of disappointment in her voice.

"Well, I hope you'll let me help next time," Marco said warmly, his brown eyes twinkling as he winked at her. Lola felt a warmth begin to spread through her body as she smiled shyly and lowered her gaze. "Listen," he continued, "coincidence or not, these murders... they're not pointing *at* you, but if I'm being honest, I think it has something to do with your antique shop. There's a connection there, and quite frankly, I don't think everyone is happy you're back and they're trying to pin these murders on you."

Lola didn't know what to say. On one hand she didn't want to believe someone was framing her. However, her brain could only focus on one thing: did Marco like her?

Marco gently took her hand in his and looked deeply into her eyes. His gaze was intense, yet comforting, as if he knew what she was thinking and feeling.

"Lola, I want to tell you something," he said seriously. "I don't think you're the killer." He squeezed her hand reassuringly before continuing.

I've been observing you throughout the entire tour and I've seen how you react to things. You're a sensitive, honest, and kind person. You don't have the profile of someone capable of cold-blooded murder."

Lola's heart skipped a beat as she heard his words and considered the possibility of it all. A heavy burden had been lifted off her shoulders upon hearing his honesty, yet, crap! She met his gaze once again, but her eyes shifted down and realized he had lettuce in his teeth. She wasn't sure if she should say something or not.

"You don't know how much I appreciate your words, Marco," Lola smiled.

Marco returned his own broad smile.

Lola let out a laugh, and Marco's smile grew even bigger.

"Yes, uhm... I don't want to ruin the moment, but you've got lettuce between your teeth," Lola squinted, pulling her hand free and motioning with a finger.

"Oh... uh, uhm!" mumbled Marco, releasing her hands, turning away, and using the tip of his nail to desperately free the lettuce. "So much for that egg-and-veggie wrap I tried to scarf down before meeting you." Lowering his gaze while turning red as a tomato, he cleared his throat and proceeded toward Sophia, who was thoroughly engaged with other tourists who had come into the church. He kept his back to Lola.

It's cute to see that even a man like him can blush. Lola grinned, and realized she hadn't felt *something* like this since she had arrived at Jaramillo. She walked up and whispered "thank you for today," and tuned back into Sophia's talk.

7

---·---

CHAPTER 7

"We live in eternal distraction. The truth is in front of our eyes more often than we believe, but we choose to look away from it. I always wondered why. Perhaps I understand now: there are hearts that are not prepared for the cruelty of this world. I believe I have one of those." The Killer.

The next day, Lola met with Jax, Jade, and their friends at her brother's workplace after hours. They had all agreed to meet after Lola told them she was one of the main suspects and likely being set up, as Detective Marco had shared.

Lola walked through the salon door accompanied by Jade at her heels. She was welcomed with the smell of sweet jasmine and almond oil mixed with the stale odor of hair dryers running all day.

Jax was already sitting in the waiting area, surrounded by Cristina, Lucy, and Andrea. Jax was wearing a loose shirt that revealed his long, thin arms covered in tattoos. Everyone seemed tense; no one had expected this unfortunate turn of events.

"Hi, girls," Lola greeted them, her voice faltering slightly, "Thanks for coming."

"Hi, Lola," Cristina responded gently, followed by Lucy and Andrea's lighthearted replies.

"Hi, I don't think I'm a girl," Jax said with a cocky smile.

With how dumb you are when petting me between my ears, impossible. You have the touch of a hippopotamus, Jade commented, causing Lola to let out an inappropriate laugh. The others gave her a puzzled look.

"Jax stopped by the police station to see Brandon today. He's still in custody," Cristina said, addressing the topic directly, ignoring Lola's laugh.

"How's Brandon doing?" Lola asked, sitting down in one of the plush burgundy chairs, Jade taking up a cozy spot next to Lucy's legs in an adjacent chair.

"Not good," Jax responded evenly. "He's scared and confused. He doesn't understand why he's been arrested. He says he didn't kill anyone. But he's going to be released tomorrow...they don't have enough evidence to keep him locked up."

"Do you believe him?" Lola questioned anxiously, her gaze searching each of their eyes for some answers or solace.

"Yes," Jax affirmed. "Brandon is a good kid. A bit rebellious and lonely but good from what I know. I don't think he's capable of killing his own father."

"Neither do I. I'm glad he's getting out, I guess," Andrea murmured softly. "But I don't know. The only thing I know is Lola, you are *not* the killer. What gets me is, it's like the killer intentionally wants to make you look guilty."

"That's why we have to find the real culprit," Jax chimed in, his gaze fixed on Lola as if to give her strength.

The five friends were sitting in a dimly lit room, with an ominous silence hanging in the air. Outside, the sun was slowly sinking beyond the horizon and its dim, orange light cast eerie shadows on their faces.

The only sound to be heard was the ticking of the clock, which seemed to be moving in slow motion.

"And how are we going to do it?" Lucy asked, reflecting the thoughts of everyone. She didn't look Jax in the eye - no one did - but instead her gaze wandered to the window.

"Well, we have a theory," Jax explained, and all at once the girls, even Jade, turned to him. "We believe that the killer is someone from the town who knows the victims well and their secrets, right? And, that someone has access to arsenic and knows how to use it. Someone who has a motive to kill we also know that the killer leaves behind these odd, yet poetic and mysterious haikus."

"And who would that someone be?" Cristina asked.

"We don't know yet," Lola admitted. "But we have some suspects."

Jax told them about his suspicions regarding Richard, Sara's ex-husband and Daniel's best friend, and the episode with Brandon and his father. "Brandon could be the killer; we don't know much about him, to be honest," Jax admitted with a hint of sadness in his eyes.

"Turns out we have a clue too," Lola chimed in, acknowledging the latest information Jax had given her. "Brandon used to write poetry when he was young. And he liked to write in a very abstract way."

"How do you know that?" Lucy asked, raising an eyebrow.

"His literature teacher told me," Jax replied. "I met her at the salon, and she said that Brandon was one of her most talented students, especially with poetry."

"So, are you all thinking what I am thinking?" Cristina asked, curiosity flashing in her eyes, looking first at Jax, then at Lola. "Maybe the killer was inspired by Brandon's poems to commit his crimes, perhaps it could be Richard," she continued. "Maybe the killer knew Brandon and stole his poems. Maybe the killer wanted to frame Brandon for his crimes. Or maybe it's him," she gloated as all eyes turned to her with surprise.

The streetlights outside the window began to glow against the darkening sky, casting their awakening shadows across the room. Jax held his gaze steady on Cristina, slightly tilting his head, pondering all she had just rambled off.

"So, for now, the suspects are..." he began.

"Richard, if he managed to kill under 'investigation'. The Detective didn't seem convinced by that surveillance. Or, it's Brandon and he committed a murder to cover up the murder he really wanted to do, or... I don't know. Maybe none of them," Cristina resigned, slumping back in the chair, crossing her arms and eyeing Lola before quickly looking away.

"We're missing something," Lola replied firmly, her eyes narrowing slightly in thought as she spoke, looking at no one but the growing shadows.

Jax nodded in agreement. "We are," he said, with absolute resolve.

***

Two days had passed and the investigation didn't seem to be making any progress. Everyone was wary of Brandon, Richard, and at times, even Lola; to the point of avoiding them all together. The city seemed to have gone quiet on the streets and the charm of summer was slowly fading away.

Lola was painstakingly cleaning an old piece of furniture in the back of the antique store while Charles, her only employee for the moment, had gone out to buy a soda. She expected him to be back any minute, since the soda shop was just around the corner, and it was his turn to cover the front counter; instead, she heard hard fast footsteps coming from the entrance.

"Lola, eh... LOLA!" Charles shouted from far away, sounding panicked.

Putting down the chemicals, securing them tightly and removing her glove with a snap of the rubber catching on her skin, Lola pushed herself up off the stool and headed toward the front. "What's up, Charles?" Lola asked, a little concerned.

"Did you know that a truck could have driven through the store and you wouldn't have even noticed," Charles teased.

"Charles..."

"On an island like this, I bet you could mistake a tornado for a tsunami," he gestured wildly.

"Charles..."

"When it comes to the attention span of goldfish..."

"CHARLES!" Lola snapped, interrupting his ramblings of nonsense.

"I'm sorry, sometimes I can't stop making bad jokes when I'm nervous," Charles confessed, rubbing his hands together, the can crinkling under his palm causing Lola to realize he had a death grip on the poor soda can.

"You see, um, there's been another murder," Charles said nervously and Lola's world tilted.

8

— ❖ —

CHAPTER 8

"*I guess a part of me wants to be discovered. Some will say it's ego, but I know it's appreciation for my work. The art of deception has come more easily to me than writing. Perhaps I am a reflection of humanity: arrogant, conceited, and dangerous, but extremely talented.*" The Killer.

Three days after the last murder, Lola, Jax, Cristina, Lucy, Andrea, Jade and Marco gathered at Lola's place after work, with the moon already setting in the town's sky over the island. A light mist in the air made the ocean air hazy and ominous.

The detective had shown up at Lola's house to talk to her alone, as the media wasn't releasing details about the latest murder. However, he thought it was a good idea to join the group to talk a bit with everyone and get to know them. So, there he was, as one of the others, although he stood out in the living room like a crow among pigeons, the night at the bar long forgotten.

The town was in chaos, and with a serial killer loose on its streets, the group actually felt a little safer with a detective around. The haikus murders were international news now. Many looked at Lola with fear or even anger. She tried to ignore it: proving her innocence was all she thought about, not coincidences. On the antique glass table, there was a pile of papers with newspaper clippings about the killer's haikus and the notes everyone had taken as they came up with ideas.

Lola frowned and ran a hand through her loose wavy hair that was usually pulled back in a bun.

"Brandon could be the killer; we don't know much about him, to be honest," Jax admitted.

No one responded. Everyone's eyes were everywhere, avoiding direct contact with anyone.

"It doesn't make sense," Lola declared, breaking the heavy silence that hung in the air. "Why would Brandon kill his own father with the same method and the same type of poem as Daniel's killer? And who the heck is this Annie, the new victim?"

"The customer who didn't get her watch," Jax answered, staring coldly at his sister.

Cristina piped up from her corner of the couch. "Maybe he wanted to throw the police off," she suggested. "Or maybe he was working with someone else to also kill this Annie person."

Lucy chimed in with a question directed at Lola, "And then who do you think is guilty?"

Still reeling from Jax's comment, Lola stammered, "Ri-Richard. For now, I think anyway," she hesitated then continued. "He had a motive to kill Daniel, and he could have sent someone to kill Randall to throw off suspicion. It wouldn't be that complicated," she conceded.

Andrea turned away from her friends and looked at Marco and Jax skeptically as she snipped. "That's a bit of a stretch, Lola. Richard was under surveillance, even if Marco isn't convinced. Besides, he's not capable of writing those haikus. He's a bad writer according to Jax."

"And are you any good?" Marco asked Jax with a smile, tilting his head towards him. "We all think you're excellent, but you've never shown us anything." Marco continued, without allowing him to answer, "Unofficially, because you didn't get it from me, here's the haiku the killer left behind. Maybe *you* have some insights about it to share, huh?" Marco slipped him a folded piece of paper.

Lola narrowed her eyes at Marco with suspicion. It seemed strange to her that he was asking such a direct question to her brother like that. Marco could be so bold... probably why he's a detective.

Before Jax could respond, Marco turned to Lola. She couldn't tell if Marco's social conduct was a result of his detective tactics or if he was simply making casual conversation.

"Lola, can I talk to you for a moment?" Marco asked, getting up. "We need to speak privately."

Jade let out a low growl, lifting her head.

"Sure," Lola said, first looking at the others before following him to the door. "What's going on?"

"Please," Marco gestured, leading out of the loft and down the spiral staircase and out the back door leading to the street, stopping on the sidewalk. The light of a waning moon cast eerie shadows upon them. The night was still and silent, except for the rustling of palm leaves in the trees. Marco stood tall, his face grim as he looked into Lola's eyes. She had a look of fear on her face, her body tense with uncertainty.

"Lola," Marco began, "I have to tell you something important."

"What?" Lola asked nervously, her voice quivering slightly. "Is there any news in the case that you have to tell me away from the others?"

"Yes, there is news," Marco said regretfully, looking towards the moon. "And it's not good for you."

Lola took a step back from him, her eyes wide in disbelief. "What do you mean? Have they found evidence against me?"

"Not exactly. But the police believe that you are the prime suspect in the murders."

Lola gasped sharply, her hand frozen in midair as if she were about to ward off an evil spirit. She stood motionless and speechless, staring at Marco. She slowly sat down on the curb, her hands shaking. She gathered her breath and asked, "Why? What evidence do they have?"

"They don't have concrete evidence," Marco said honestly. "But they have ruled out the other suspects for lack of it. Brandon has a solid alibi for the third crime since being released, and for the first, but they're still investigating him for the second. Richard, on the other hand, was already under investigation during the second and third. Although I doubt how much attention they were paying to him when Randall was killed." Marco took a seat next to her on the sandy curb, wrapping his arms around his legs, letting go of the breath that was stuck in his chest.

"You're the only one left by elimination," Marco said sadly. "Circumstantial really. You arrived in town just as the murders started. You saw the three victims before they died. You're a known writer…"

"What? When did I see Annie?" Lola gasped, panic lacing her voice. Except, she had seen Annie. Annie was the customer Jax referred to who had recently passed through the store. She had been the one who had the 1930 English pocket watch on hold, prompting an argument between Charles and Jax.

"But that's not enough to accuse me," Lola exclaimed. "I have no motive to kill those people. I have nothing to do with them."

Marco turned towards her, seeing the fear in her eyes as she looked at him. "I know," he said softly, "and I believe you."

It was as if Marco's words soothed Lola's racing heart as they comforted her like warm hugs of love. She felt tears prickling behind her eyes and blinked them back furiously, looking away down the alley.

Taking advantage of this momentary reprieve, Marco took one of Lola's hands gently in his own. She shuddered slightly at his touch, but it helped to ground her as he smiled sweetly and spoke, "Don't worry, I'll help you get through this. Trust me."

A beam of moonlight cast a soft radiance on the two figures. Lola's heart was fluttering as if it was going to fly out of her chest. Marco's jaw was clenched tight like he was trying to rein in his emotions - they looked in opposite directions.

Crying out in the silence, Marco's phone buzzed, ending the awkward exchange. Marco grunted as he stood, slightly frustrated with the interruption, and took the phone out of his pocket, looking at the Caller ID.

"Sorry, I have to answer," he said. "It's my sister."

Lola nodded, and bit her lower lip, placing her hands in her lap. She wondered what would have happened if the phone hadn't rung.

Marco put the phone to his ear walking a few feet away into the alley.

When he hung up the phone, Lola looked at him curiously and asked as he strolled back towards her, "Did something happen?"

"No," Marco replied without giving any details.

Lola nodded understandingly and didn't insist, pulling herself up.

Lola felt that there was something between them, something more that made them feel something other than nervousness amid so much death.

Marco hesitated, "It's time for me to go. I have a lot to do tomorrow."

Lola nodded sheepishly and watched him walk away as he headed towards his car, got behind the wheel, started the engine, and sped away.

Lola stood alone at the back door, on the landing of the curb to the shop staring at the void left by Marco. She put her hand on her chest and felt her heart still racing. Whether it was because she was a suspect or a possible love interest, she wasn't sure, but when she felt the fur around her ankles, she knew who had come to find her. Jade's tail twitched in agitation.

He still reeks of death... he's too close.

9

---·---

CHAPTER 9

"Time is relative. It can seem like an eternity or a fleeting moment. But what matters is not the time itself, but what we do with it. I have chosen to dedicate my life to creating this work that will transcend time and space. What is life if we do not leave a mark on this world?" The Killer.

The next day, Lola and her friends met again at Lola's house. It was Sunday and they could afford to spend some uninterrupted time together, given what was happening. Jax joined them, walking in with Jade in his arms even though she was meowing impatiently. Lola sat on the black love seat and continued working on the sweater; she was already halfway done.

"Hey, girls. Any news since last night?" Jax greeted with a forced smile, closing the door behind him.

"Yeah, we've discovered the killer, but we're having coffee before going to the police, since the detective just left us," Cristina responded sarcastically.

"What do you think about the latest haiku the killer left, Jax?" Lucy asked curiously.

"It doesn't make sense to me," he said, frowning.

"Let's read it again," Andrea suggested, taking out her phone, handing it to Lola.

"Snake's venomous touch,

So soft and deceptive skin,

Lethal bite for her,"

"What does that mean? And what does it have to do with Annie?" Lucy wondered.

"No idea. It's very abstract and cryptic. This one is better written though. The killer has been practicing," Jax admitted.

"Maybe it's a metaphor. Maybe the killer means that life is like a snake's poison that kills us slowly," Cristina proposed.

"Or maybe it's a word game. I don't know, the problem is not knowing anything about Annie. Everything indicates that she was a normal girl," Andrea surmised.

"Or maybe it's a clue about the killer's identity. Maybe it's an ego thing, like he wants people to know who he is," Lola suggested, fixing another mistake within the sleeve she was sure she fixed already.

"I don't know, but I can ask the ladies at the hair salon about Annie. They surely know everything," Jax said, rolling his eyes, crossing his leg in the chair opposite of Lola.

While the humans continued to argue about the killer's haiku, Jade grew bored and distracted by the smells and sounds of the kitchen, where Lucy was preparing coffee for everyone. The faint scent of an apple pie coming out of the kitchen overwhelmed Jade's senses, making her mouth water. Jade literally was drooling onto her paw, watching the people in the room.

Lola, can you give me a piece of that cake that smells so good? Jade mumbled to Lola.

"What cake?" Lola asked, aloud, hyper-focused on the cumbersome stitch, not understanding.

The one in the kitchen. The one that smells like apple, explained Jade.

Lola looked up from her project, her head snapping towards the kitchen, becoming faintly aware of the mouth-watering aroma through Jade. *Oh, that cake. I think Jax brought it, and it's important to him. He told me we would eat it on Wednesday to celebrate some news he wants to share with me,* Lola replied mentally, returning to her work.

Why is that? Is he more important than me? Jade scoffed, audibly.

No, of course not. But he asked me specifically, saying he wants us to celebrate as siblings. Besides, the cake may not be good for you, reasoned Lola.

Pfftt, cake is good for everyone. It's sweet and delicious, Jade added with a sorrowful meow, *And I deserve it more than anyone else. I'm the only one who eats almost the same food every day,* Jade insisted.

Lola sighed and tried to ignore her whining cat. She focused on her friends' conversation, and she realized then that all eyes were on her.

"And tell me, Lola, how are things going with Detective Marco?" Cristina teasingly asked, leaning forward on the couch.

"With Marco? Well, good, I guess," Lola replied, blushing.

"Come on, Lola, don't play dumb. We know you like Marco. It shows in the way you look at him," Lucy said with a coy smile, serving up the coffee on an ornate silver tray.

"How? No, I don't look at him in any particular way," Lola defended herself nervously.

"Yes, you do. You look at him with those lovestruck eyes," Andrea chimed in, batting her eyelashes.

"That's not true. I just...it's like... oh c'mon," Lola stuttered.

"He's a very handsome and friendly man, you might as well go for it," Cristina advised. "What did he want anyway when you two left, anyway?"

"Nothing, really," Lola lied. "I mean...yes, I don't deny that he's friendly, but he's also very mysterious and reserved." She returned her attention away from her friends, intentionally focusing again on her crocheting, avoiding their stares.

"That makes him more interesting. Besides, I'm sure he's a good investigator since the local police brought him in from the mainland," mused Lucy.

"Yes, but he's also very distrustful, I think," pointed out Andrea.

Jade listened attentively to the human conversation and thought to herself: *Death lingers around Marco. And Lola. And he smells bad, like a wet dog*, Jade thought with disdain, but it went unnoticed by Lola, who was reflecting on Andrea's comment. There was something about it that made her doubt Marco's true intentions for being on the island. "I wonder if he has ulterior motives with me," Lola said honestly.

"You better hope so!" Cristina quipped. "But not if you're in jail," she said seriously.

"I'm afraid you're not too far off, Cris," Lola whispered. One more stitch. "This killer won't stop pointing things towards me," Lola confessed.

No cake will be the death of me.

Jade grew impatient. She decided to take matters into her own hands and started sauntering towards the kitchen, walking over to Jax's feet.

"Hey, where's Jade going?" Jax asked, watching the cat walk away.

"I don't know; she must have seen something that caught her attention," Lola replied, thankful for Jade's distraction.

"Well, you should keep an eye on her. She might get into trouble," Jax warned, standing up.

Lola looked at her cat and saw that she was near the kitchen door. She knew exactly what she wanted.

"Jade! Come here! You can't go in there!" Lola insisted, tossing down the sweater, and clumsily clamoring out of the sofa.

Jade ignored Lola and opened the swinging door with her paw. She entered the kitchen and headed for the counter where the apple cake was. She swung her tail twice and lurched upwards, but a hand snatched her, her paws landing on nothing but air.

"JADE! I brought this pie to celebrate my promotion at the salon," Jax said angrily, clearly disappointed at apparently revealing the surprise.

"I'm sorry, Jax!" Lola apologized. "JADE!" she scolded her cat.

I didn't eat it. It smells rotten deep inside. But, if I had wanted to eat it, no human would have been able to catch me, Jade replied, proud and defiant.

Shaking her head at her very determined cat, Lola came back into the living room with Jax close behind, disappointed for having revealed his promotion too soon to his sister.

"We have to prove Lola's innocence. Tomorrow, I'll talk to the ladies at the salon, and they'll surely give us some key information," Jax continued, giving Jade a sour look as he continued, "Mrs. Nodis never shuts up about anything or anybody, and she has an appointment tomorrow. That woman...I hope it's not something as terrible as last time. I'm almost embarrassed to cut her hair."

The girls snickered, exchanging glances. Jade yawned while taking it upon herself to snag a couple pieces of yarn dangling from the side of the basket while Lola resumed crocheting. Everyone, including Jade, thought Jax had a good idea.

They all agreed that Lola would go to Jax's workplace at the end of his shift and see if Mrs. Nodis or any of the other ladies had any information.

***

On Monday, as the sunset bathed the treetops, Lola made her way to Jax's workplace, eagerly awaiting news. Once they met up, they started their walk around closing the businesses while Jax began to recount what he had learned from the ladies at the salon, led by Mrs. Nodis.

"Apparently, Annie had a secret boyfriend," Jax told Lola. "No one knew who he was or what his name was. They just knew he was very wealthy and gave her expensive gifts."

"Don't you find that suspicious? Maybe that boyfriend is the killer. Or maybe she wanted to break up with him and he found out. Or he was married, and she was blackmailing him," Lola said a little too excitedly.

"We need to find some answers that lead us to whoever 'he' is to be able to answer any of those questions, dear sister. Something that tells us his name or what he does for a living."

Just then, an older woman approached them from behind and touched their shoulders, startling them both. "Excuse me. I'm so sorry, but, please, I beg you...can I talk to you for a moment?" she asked with a sweet but nervous voice.

Lola and Jax turned around and saw Sophia, the town's travel agent. Lola recognized her instantly. "Hi Sophia," Lola greeted her. "How are you?"

"Hi Lola," Sophia replied with a worried look. "I'm fine, thank you."

"What did you want to tell us? Oh, and this is my brother, Jax," Lol gestured, smiling.

"Hello," Sophia glanced briefly at Jax, eyeing the tattoos exposed on his arms. "Listen, I have to tell you something very important. Something that has to do with ...*the murders*," she whispered, even though no one was close enough to hear.

"With the murders?" Jax repeated. "And what do you know about the murders?"

"I know," Sophia whispered, leaning toward the twins. "I know who the killer is," Sophia insisted, grabbing Lola's forearm. "And I know where he lives and what he does for a living."

10

— · —

CHAPTER 10

"There are fingers that will point at me like a monster. There are fingers that will point at me like someone who made justice an art." The Killer.

Lola and Jax were stunned. They couldn't believe what they had just heard. How could Sophia know who the killer was? And why did she want to tell them? How did she know *anything*?

Sophia noticed their surprise and motioned for them to follow her. "Come with me," she said. "I'll explain everything at my house. It's safer there. There are too many people here, and we might be watched."

"No, wait," protested Jax, grabbing her sleeve. "We can't just go with you like that. How do we know you're not lying or deceiving us? What proof do you have of what you're saying?"

"Enough to at least consider listening to me," the woman snapped back out of fear.

Sophia looked at them both, her eyes wild, darting to and fro. Even though Jax had his doubts, Lola couldn't miss the opportunity to prove her own innocence.

"It's fine, Sophia, we'll come with you," Lola eyed Jax, nodding her head for him to agree.

"Yeah, yeah, okay, let's go already."

The three of them headed to Sophia's house, which was only a few blocks away. It was a small and cozy house decorated with the native island's flowers and vines, framing the entryway. Sophia opened the door and invited them in.

"Welcome to my humble abode," said Sophia, seemingly more comfortable now that they were off the streets. "Please, have a seat on the couch. I'll bring you something to drink."

Lola and Jax sat on the small leather couch and looked around the inside of the house. There were photos of travels from all over the world, books in different languages, and souvenirs from various countries.

"Wow, Sophia," remarked Jax. "It looks like you've traveled a lot."

Sophia returned with a tray of three cups of coffee and some pastries.

"Yes, I've been lucky enough to see many places and cultures," said Sophia as she sat the coffee in front of her guests. "But now, I'm happy to live here on this quiet and beautiful island."

Lola took a cup and pretended to take a sip, but she didn't actually drink any.

"Sophia, can you tell us why you brought us here?" Lola asked quietly.

Sophia sighed and looked at them seriously, holding her own coffee cup, trembling slightly.

Lola and Jax leaned forward, expectantly.

Before Sophia could answer, Lola's phone started ringing and interrupted the woman. It was Andrea. The time was 7:07 - Andrea was supposed to feed Jade at 7:00, the time Jade always ate, so that she wouldn't get...*catty*. However, if everything was alright, Andrea would have sent her a message. The fact that she was making a video call surprised her.

"Sorry, I have to take this call," she said to the others, setting down her coffee before standing and moving towards the front door.

Lola answered, "Hello, Andrea. Is everything alright?"

"Hey, Lola. I fed Jade, but she's acting very strangely. That's why I'm calling you."

"How strange? Jade is already strange enough."

"She keeps jumping, scratching and biting me, running from one place to another and staring at me. I think she wants to...to talk to you in some way. Hold on, I'll put her on video call, get this crazy cat under control, will ya?" Andrea pleaded.

Jade appeared, taking up the entire screen of the phone. First, she sniffed it, then she looked directly to where Lola should have been on Andrea's phone.

I needed to talk to you, Lola. It's very important, almost as important as you remembering to buy some fish on the way back. And a new scratcher.

What's going on? Lola asked, laughing a little on the inside, but ignoring Jade's requests.

I've found evidence that leads us directly to the killer, and I'm sorry to say that it is...

At that moment, Jade froze at first, then hissed, getting into an attack position.

"Jade! What's going on?" Lola said out loud in panic?

"Oh no," said Jax, looking over his shoulder at her.

Lola stared at Jade, not realizing what was going on. Then she saw him. She looked over her shoulder towards the opposite side of the room. Looking back at her phone, she could see him in the corner of the screen that her visage didn't cover.

A black cat was licking its paw.

Jade stared at it intently and was beside herself. The other cat, which Sophia called over to keep it from bothering them, was named Michi and was totally unaware of the situation. He had been grooming himself in the background of Lola's phone, now strutting over to his owner who was eager to give him some chin scratching.

When Sophia picked him up the cat let out a soft "meow," Jade came to herself.

"Jade, you were saying..."

WHAT ARE YOU DOING WITH ANOTHER CAT? WHO IS THAT CAT? WHAT DOES IT SMELL LIKE? YOU'RE GONE FOR ONE AFTERNOON AND YOU'RE ALREADY PETTING ANOTHER...

"Jade! Focus on what's important!" Lola hissed back, not wanting to yell at Jade.

NOW YOU'LL COME BACK SMELLING LIKE ANOTHER CAT, I BET YOU WERE SCRATCHING ITS BELLY. DOES IT EVEN KNOW YOUR NAME? I CAN'T BELIEVE IT, IF...

Lola realized it was a lost cause and that once Jade started on a tirade, there's no stopping her...without tuna. Later she would buy her lots of fish and toys to try and get this other cat out of her mind. Who knew a cat could be so insanely jealous?

She told Andrea to end the call, as she smiled briefly, sitting back down next to Jax who gave her a puzzled look. Sophia looked at her strangely but continued on.

Sophia raised her cup back to her lips, sipped, and looked at them with worry in her eyes.

"I think the killer is... Marco," Sophia whispered with a trembling voice - even though no one else was in the room.

Lola and Jax were stunned by Sophia's accusation.

"Marco? Are you sure?" Lola asked incredulously.

Sophia nodded firmly.

"Yes, I'm sure. Marco is the killer. And he's going to try to frame *me!*" Sophia cried with anguish.

Lola and Jax looked at each other in confusion.

"But... why? What in the world would make you think that?" Jax asked skeptically.

Sophia took a sip of coffee again and told them her story. "A few days ago, Marco came to my agency to question me about the first murder. He said it was routine, that he wanted to know if I had seen anything suspicious or if I knew the taxi driver, Daniel. I told him no, that I had only seen him once when he took me to the airport a few months ago. But Marco didn't seem to believe me. He asked me many questions about my past, even about my ex-husband," Sophia seemed rather bitter about the last part.

Jax tensed up at the reminder of the rumor he had heard at the salon about Sophia and her ex-husband.

"What happened with your ex-husband?" Lola asked delicately.

Sophia sighed and started petting the cat who was now curled up in her lap, blinking slowly, purring his contentment. "My ex-husband was a monster. He abused me physically for years," she said, her voice low and trembling. "He made my life impossible. Nobody helped me, nobody listened to me. But yet, everyone *knew* what I was going through, they just refused to help," Sophia stated with contempt, a hint of anger in her voice. Michi hardly noticed his owner's demeanor change.

Lola felt compassion for her, but Jax boldly asked, "And what happened to your ex-husband?"

Sophia didn't even flinch and said in a flat voice, "I killed him," Sophia confessed without remorse, "with arsenic."

The twins stared at her in shock.

"No one investigated the case. No one cared. He was an old, surly man and they all assumed it was a natural death," Sophia held their gaze for another moment then looked down at her coffee, taking a huge gulp. "Don't worry, I haven't killed anyone else. I'm not this haiku killer. Heck, I think it's Marco wanting to make sure that when he reveals what really happened to my ex-husband, then no one will suspect him. Which then turns all eyes on me."

Lola and Jax shared a troubled look.

Sophia continued, her hands shaking, holding the coffee cup, "Some big hotshot detective coming to our island would gain so much publicity as a detective for solving this case. A case that *he* practically invented by tying the murders together. He's the only one who benefits from all of this!" She cried, meeting their green eyes once again before continuing, "Marco asked me to have coffee, alone, next Friday. I think he plans to finish putting the pieces together and then will arrest me."

"What about the haikus?" Lola asked, her voice barely audible.

"Oh, that's the best part," she chuckled. "I have been passionate about Eastern literature since my trip to Japan in 1985. In my library, you will find many books on the subject, and I have been writing haikus for many years, as a hobby. I'm the *perfect* suspect, once the secret of my ex-husband is revealed."

An uncomfortable silence blanketed the room sending chills down Lola's spine. Sophia continued, as if she was speaking both her confessions and prideful defense into her coffee cup, "But it's impossible for me to be the killer...I wouldn't have been so careless to begin with. The murder I committed proves that. Those haikus...are *very* poorly written, "she scoffed, "they're...juvenile...to say the least."

Lola was perplexed, Jax seemed taken aback. Sofia held their gaze, shifting from one pair of emerald eyes to the next. The kindness of the person who had first shown Lola around the town with Marco had suddenly disappeared; in its place was this cold, broken woman, her eyes darkened and unwavering.

Lola felt incredibly uneasy and wanted to run away, while Jax looked at the travel agent with deep contempt.

11

CHAPTER 11

S ophia seemed to pick up on their feelings and added with a soft voice, "I know what you must be thinking. I did what I had to do with my husband. He deserved it."

She slowly got up from her seat, unfolding her body as if trying to expand her tiny frame. She straightened her back, fixed her hair, and said with a slight smile, "Well, I better serve more coffee." Without saying anything else, she headed towards the kitchen.

Lola and Jax watched in silence as Sophia's small figure disappeared through the door that separated the living room from the kitchen and shifted uncomfortably in their seats. When their eyes met, Lola was terrified and Jax looked furious. He made a soothing gesture, and his gaze danced over to the bookshelf in the corner of the living room. His eyes landed on an open book that was there. He got up, looked at it, and sat back down. Both felt some tension in the air.

The woman returned with a full pot of coffee and as she was about to pour coffee she stopped, as if there was a reflection that made her pause.

"Don't you see? All the murders point to people who have caused harm, in one way or another. People who have done 'evil.' Haikus are about that. Daniel deceived his best friend, Randall couldn't care less about his son, Annie pretended to love her partner so he would buy her expensive gifts. That childish thought of punishing those who have done wrong is not how I work."

Sophia was about to pour them coffee before realizing their cups were still full, so she poured herself some more, set the coffee pot down and curled back up on the chair next to Michi and continued, "Evil is ambiguous, and that fool Marco must believe that he is doing good."

Sophia scoffed, looked down at Michi, met their gaze and explained, "I've read every haiku. I've made the connections. It wasn't difficult, really. The first one: 'The withered flower, deceiving of one's own self, justice blooms for them.' Marco underestimated love. He believed that love is as simple as an agreement between a couple, and condemned Daniel. He believed Daniel was 'the bad guy'. He had cheated on his best friend in some way and started a relationship with his wife *after* they divorced.

Maybe Daniel was bad, maybe not..." she shrugged and took a sip. "But 'justice blooms'? Marco has a huge ego, thinking he's capable of determining what is justice, what is evil, and what is the withered flower?'" Sophia placed the coffee pot on the table, sighed, shook her head, and made a face.

Then she took a few breaths before continuing. "Then came the murder of Brandon's father. What was his name?" she asked looking puzzled.

"Randall," Lola replied in a low voice, subtly moving her cup away from Sophia so she wouldn't insist she drink up.

"Right, Randall," Sophia muttered, thoughtful, tapping her lips as if she were thinking. "I understand what motivated Marco with Randall. Abandoning a child like that is cruel, without a doubt..." She stood up, suddenly, startling Michi. She walked to the library case, then around the desk next to it, and rummaged through some papers and newspapers. She returned with a newspaper in her hands.

"A poor orphaned soul, deprived of love and guidance, guilt eats him alive," she recited. "I think it's clear. On the one hand, it's about Brandon, the man deprived of a father. On the other hand, the guilt Randall *should* feel. The damage Randall did is unspeakable. Being an absent father is not something that can be remedied overnight. The lack of love and guidance is something that will be tattooed on his soul.

"I suppose Marco wanted Randall to feel the same, to feel damaged. But an irreversible damage: death." She threw the newspaper on the table and looked at her hands. "There's no doubt, an absent father is damaging to a child, yet who did Marco think he was to judge?" she asked, looking Jax in the eye.

"And then there's Annie... a coy lady with her charm, victim of a man's strange morality," Sophia continued, as if reciting poetry.

"How do you know about Annie?" Jax asked, shooting to his feet, sounding almost too demanding.

Sophia paused for a moment, furrowing her brow at him. "You're not the only ones who have been looking for answers, dear boy."

"Snake's venomous touch, so soft and deceptive skin, lethal bite for her," the woman quoted, looking at her visitors. Jax sat back down, picking up a scone from the tray, not taking his eyes off the woman. Lola sneezed, though it sounded like a disguised "let's go."

Jax put his hand on her knee, indicating for her to wait.

"For Marco, Annie was a snake, slowly poisoning her lover with a ...toxic and deadly charm. She took advantage of the man's tender heart in order to take advantage of his wallet. But Marco, self-defining as justice, gave her a taste of her own medicine and poisoned her. Plus, this murder was super convenient to incriminate me since it's the same method I used to kill my husband," Sophia concluded and settled back into her chair as if she had finished a long and complicated speech.

A minute of uncomfortable silence passed, and only then did she look at them. "So, what now?"

"We're leaving," announced Lola, standing up, unexpectedly.

"You haven't tried my coffee," Sophia said innocently, looking at Lola and Jax in turn.

"We wouldn't drink coffee from a killer, Sophia," Jax replied, furious.

"Why in the world would you tell us all of this, Sophia?" Lola asked.

"Because when all of this is revealed, and you see how things unfold, I can trust that you will help me. When Marco pretends to be a hero you will be my voice of truth. And I know, Lola, that the distrust that everyone has towards you, even though you haven't done anything, is what will motivate you to help me. I'm sorry for using you in this way, but I'm old and I just want to live out my best years," Sophia pleaded.

"Or maybe you wanted to kill us for checking it out. Or at least, divert our attention," Lola said, pointing to the coffee.

"Only time will reveal the truth, dear twins. See you soon," Sophia said, sipping her coffee.

12

CHAPTER 12

"*There are stories that are read between the lines. If you have read my work, if you paid attention, you should already know who the monster is.*" The Killer.

Lola and Jax left Sophia's house feeling uneasy and suspicious. The old woman had told them a story that had left them shaken and confused. According to her, Marco was the haiku killer and was trying to incriminate her for an old rumor circulating on the island.

If what Sophia said was true, that Marco was very dangerous and was digging up the past, was he digging into each of them? "What do you think about what Sophia told us?" Lola asked Jax as they walked down the street.

"I don't believe it for a second," Jax replied firmly. "I think she's a liar and a killer."

"Why do you say that?"

"Because it makes sense, Lola. Think about it. Why would she have invited us to her house if she had nothing to hide? Why would she have told us that strange story about Marco? Doesn't that seem too convenient to you?"

"Well, maybe she just wanted to warn us. Maybe Marco really is the culprit."

"I don't think so, Lola. I think Sophia is trying to divert our attention away from herself and trying to get us on her side when she's caught. I suppose Marco has gotten too close. I really believe that she's the haiku killer."

"How do you know?"

"For several reasons. First, because she admitted she killed her ex-husband through arsenic poisoning. Second, because she's bitter about life in general, which makes her suspicious, getting back at people because she just can. And third, because she knows how to write Japanese poetry," Jax concluded.

"How do you know the last one?"

"Because I saw it in her house. She had several poetry books on her bookshelf, and one of them was open to a page with a haiku. That's what I was reading while she was getting coffee"

"A haiku? Are you sure, Jax?"

"Yes, Lola. I read it myself. It was something like:

"Life is a dream time,

That fades at dawn, crushed by night,"

Only dust remains."

That one, Lola... was about a sad love story. A woman who falls in love, but is killed by her lover, only to realize none of them ever truly lived.

"Wow," Lola murmured, slowing her pace, thinking, "That's right, she mentioned how she thought the writing was juvenile, and she's been *studying* books on haikus alone."

"Yes, see what I mean?" Jax affirmed. "And there's more. Remember what Sophia told us about Marco? That he knew a lot about her past and about the rumors surrounding her ex-husband?"

"Yes..."

"Well, don't you find it strange that Marco would know that? Where would he have gotten that information?"

"I don't know... maybe from the police or a background check? Don't detectives do that sort of thing?"

"I don't think so," Jax said matter-of-factly. "If he did, we would know. He would have told *you,* don't you think?"

Lola blushed at Jax's words. It was true that she felt something for Marco, even though she didn't want to admit it. But it was also true that there was something about him that made her doubt. Something in his gaze, his voice, his attitude. Something that made her think he was hiding a secret. "I don't know what to think, Jax," Lola said, puzzled by all of it. "I don't know who to believe anymore."

"Believe me, Lola," Jax said tenderly. "I'm your brother. I love you."

Lola looked at Jax with gratitude and affection. He was her twin, her confidant, her best friend. He had always been by her side, supporting and encouraging her while growing up. He had always been her partner in literary adventures, struggling to make it big as a bestselling author. He had always been her hero - even when he failed.

"I trust you, Jax," Lola said with a smile. "I trust you."

Jax returned the smile and gave her a nuggie on the head.

"C'mon, let's go look for Marco," Jax said. "I gotta stop by my house and drop off these work receipts; you meet up with Andrea and check on that darn cat of yours, okay? Then we'll meet directly at the hotel where Marco is staying. We'll tell him what Sophia told us. He's our biggest source of information and if what Sophia says is true, which I don't believe, he'll reveal himself in some way. We should go to him as a first measure, he'll know what to do. Meet me there, ok?"

Lola nodded and they parted ways.

***

Upon arriving at the hotel where Marco was staying, they found that he wasn't there. There was no sign of the detective, not even his car was parked at the entrance. Lola and Jax knocked on the door several times, but no one answered. Lola took out her cell phone and dialed Marco's number, but she only heard the ringing tone with no answer.

"Where could he be?" Lola asked with concern.

"I don't know. Maybe he went out to run some errands," Jax suggested.

"Or maybe..." Lola didn't dare to finish her sentence.

At that moment, Lola noticed that she had a missed call and a text message from Cristina. She opened the message and was left speechless after reading it.

"What's going on?" Jax asked after seeing Lola's expression.

"It's Cristina. She says that Sophia has been murdered. She was driving by on her way home when she saw police cars parked around her house...they were removing a body from the home."

13

—·—

CHAPTER 13

"*O*nly one thing could inflict a mortal wound on me: leaving my work incomplete. I've come so far, I'm so close...*" The Killer.

Lola and Jax walked quickly back towards Sophia's house. It was already late, but neighbors were coming out to see what the commotion was all about. They too were just discovering that Sophia, the travel agent who had been a large part of their community, had been found dead in her home with a haiku on her chest. The police had arrived on the scene, but Detective Marco was nowhere to be seen.

Cristina was there and kept them informed of everything. Lola and Jax didn't know what to think. Could it be possible that Marco was the culprit? Lola and Jax decided to go back to the shop and weigh their options before speaking to anyone.

Cristina, somehow had an 'inside man' and sent them the haiku, which had already leaked to the press:

"Fluttering white wings,

Branch that burdens underweight,

Reaction of flight."

Jax frowned as he read the haiku and let out a chuckle. "How ironic. Sophia thought she was smarter than the killer and, in the end, she ended up like the others. She deserved it for getting involved where she wasn't needed."

Lola looked at him with shock and disbelief.

"What are you saying, Jax? How can you talk like that about a dead woman we just saw? Sophia only wanted to help us. She told us she suspected Marco."

"Sure, and that's why he killed her, right? Because she was a good Samaritan who wanted to save us from an evil detective. Please, Lola. Don't be naive. Sophia was a witch who meddled in other people's lives. She probably had something to do with the murders, like I suspected."

"What? What are you talking about, Jax? What's gotten into you? You sound like a different person."

Jax tensed up and stood up from the couch.

"Nothing's wrong with me, Lola. I'm just being realistic. We can't trust anyone. Only ourselves. And Jade, of course. By the way, where is she?"

"I don't like how you're talking, Jax. No one *deserves* to die. Sophia was sweet, she wasn't evil. She was just scared."

"Scared? Of what?"

Irritated with her brother, Lola snapped, "I don't know, he killer, perhaps?"

Jax fell silent and looked at her with a strange expression.

"Look, Lola. Sorry, okay? I'm just saying that we shouldn't trust anyone. Not even Marco."

"I don't know who to trust...I *want* to believe he wants to help us, but..."

"Does he want to help you, or does he want you, Lola?"

Lola blushed and looked down. "I don't know what you're talking about, Jax. Marco seems like a good man. I think he wants to help all of us."

Jax laughed and approached Lola who was on the black loveseat.

"How do you know he doesn't lie to you? Are you sure about that, Lola? Are you sure he's not hiding something from *you*? Something important?"

Lola looked at him with fear and confusion. "What do you mean, Jax? What is Marco hiding from me?"

Jax smiled and whispered in her ear. "He suspects *you*."

At that moment, there was an unexpected knock at the front door of Lola's loft, followed by a burst of wood splintering into the air. Detective Marco and a police officer appeared a second later, the latter wielding his gun.

"You, you piece of garbage," Marco spat, about to lunge at Jax, but his partner put a hand on his shoulder.

"Wait, Marco. Jax, hands where I can see them. You're under arrest, charged with 4 counts of murder," the police officer announced sternly, his dark eyes, never wavering.

"Wha..what's going on!?" exclaimed Jax and Lola, almost simultaneously.

Jax raised his hands, but when the officer approached to handcuff him, Jax managed to run towards the entrance with a face Lola had never seen before. The police officer was faster and tackled him, pinning him down and handcuffing him in mere seconds.

"Marco! Wha, what is going on?" Lola screamed, scared. "Jax is *innocent!* You're the..." Lola, on the verge of a breakdown, buckled and crumpled to the floor. Jade was instantly at her side, hissing, spatting, and growling...

I smelled death, it was all over you.

"Killer? Yes, that's what I asked Sophia to tell you, before your brother killed her," Marco stated, crouching down to steady her, unaware of Jade's comment.

"What?"

"Sophia's death was a trap, set up by me and the local police. You never asked me who hired me to work on this case. It was Sophia. Your brother killed her minutes after you spoke to her,' Marco choked, visibly upset that he didn't protect her.

But Lola was not in a position to listen to explanations, nor were the police officer and detective able to give them at that moment. Jade hissed once more and Jade realized it was never directly at Marco.

They took Lola to the town's police station to take her statement, and once the paperwork was done and Lola had recovered from her shock, Marco sat down with the officer in a dimly lit room facing her.

"Marco, you're making a grave mistake, Jax is not a killer!" Lola's eyes were puffy from crying and rubbing them all afternoon. Her auburn hair was disheveled and half covering her face. Jade, who made her stance at the beginning to never leave Lola's side, was at her feet, oddly still.

"Wait, Lola. Listen to me, please. And then you can make all the judgments and ask all the questions you want. The first thing you need to know is that I am not the killer, nor is Sophia. Well, scratch that, Sophia *did* kill her ex-husband, but she's not the haiku killer. Her husband was actually in a near-drowning accident - he lived, but she did everything she could to prevent him from fully recovering.

The second thing is that there is enough evidence to prove that Jax is the killer. The third thing is that your cat probably agrees with me."

"Your cat?" asked Officer Garcia, looking confused at the detective and Lola and finally Jade.

"Don't bother, Garcia. I'll explain later," Marco waved him off, "Anyway, Lola. This is the whole truth."

Marco shifted in his chair, looked sadly at Lola for a few seconds, with the pain of knowing he was about to inflict a wound that would never heal, but with the satisfaction of having saved her life.

Taking a deep breath, he started his tale. "I'm going to start from the beginning. We know that Jax planned all of this and set it in motion as soon as you stepped foot onto this island after the death of your and Jax's aunt. We are currently investigating whether she was also murdered, I'm sorry to say," Marco paused.

Lola didn't react. She had no reactions left.

He continued, "We figured his idea was to commit a series of murders that would make you look like the culprit since all of the victims had some sort of relationship with you. However, he wasn't trying to get you arrested; he wanted to see you dead. *You* were the finale of his sick plan.

"The first victim was Daniel. As you know, his best friend married his ex-wife very soon after their divorce, a rumored scandal known throughout the town. That's when I suspected both of you - during the tour with Sophia, actually.

Jade let out a piercing hiss.

Officer Garcia leapt up from his chair, startled at the bizarre sound. Lola remained unmoved. Marco rolled his eyes. "It's okay, man, you get used to it," Marco assured him, patting him on the shoulder. "That's when Jax decided that he would be the first victim, "Marco continued once the officer sat back down, further away from Jade, who was still in the same position. "He used arsenic, something you would regularly have on hand at the antique shop. He paired the poison with a haiku, since poetry is one of your writing specialties, this gave him the perfect cover."

Lola took a deep breath while Jade yawned.

"Like all the others that followed, they spoke of a certain form of karmic justice - that's what we're calling it," Marco was once again stoic as he continued. "Jax approached Daniel with the excuse of an "interview" for a book he was writing about *Redemption*. Obviously, the meeting was when Sarah, Daniel's wife, was not at home. Jax made sure that Sarah did not know who Daniel had been interviewed by, as everything was very quick, and she was working on the mainland."

"How do you know that?" Lola interrupted, meeting his gaze, her emerald eyes glassy and lifeless.

"I'll tell you. It's important you know all of it."

She lowered her eyes once more.

"The second victim was Randall. This was motivated by the violent encounter they had in your antique shop, which you witnessed. Jax knew that Richard wouldn't hold up as the main suspect for long and wanted to start shifting suspicion towards you since it was the only way for him to maintain control of the situation based on the information he would have through you and me.

"He set up another interview, this time for another type of book and character who was experiencing the same situation as Randall, an angry son and financial hardships. Jax offered him money for the interview.

"The third victim was Annie. Here, Jax wanted to throw off the investigation, we believe. He found out about Annie at the barber and hair salon after asking about that curious woman at the antique shop. Again, he offered to interview her for a character role in his book. Annie had a very big ego, so it was not difficult to trick her."

Marco paused. Looked at Garcia who just shrugged...so Marco continued, "And the last one, Sophia. At this point, I already suspected both of you. You, because of all the coincidences, and Jax, because he's your twin...perhaps, you confided in him." Marco became quiet.

Lola was motionless.

"Jax always seemed to know everything. If it wasn't because of you, it was because of the barber and hair shop. And since all the evidence pointed to a killer rather than a duo, it was very difficult to rule out your brother when you were the one we suspected. That's when he took care of that. Sophia, as I told you, was the one who hired me to come to the island - she loved this place and didn't want to see vacationers scared to come to this beautiful destination.

"As soon as she found out about the first haiku murder, she understood that due to the rumors circulating in town and her love for Eastern literature, it was only a matter of time until she was investigated and accused of the murders. So, she searched for me on the internet and contacted me.

I not only suspected you, Lola, but also Sophia. I also suspected her, but she was clean and proved it when she pretended to be a travel agent to witness my entire conversation with you. We both agreed that your brother was more suspicious than you. Then, she volunteered to set the trap for the both of you, in exchange for a reduced sentence for the murder of her husband. Sophia didn't have many years left, she just wanted to do what was right." Marco took a breath, pausing.

"Keep going."

"The idea was simple: provoke Jax or you to kill Sophia based on what she knew. Since we knew the killer's modus operandi, you know, his MO...'

"Yes, I know what that means," Lola muttered.

"Yeah, uh, so, since we knew his MO, we thought he would try and set up an interview with her. We would wait for him and catch the perpetrator in action with the arsenic.

"However, here is where the unfortunate events began. We were listening and overheard Andrea's phone call about the cat. Odd as it seems, there's *something* going on between you and Jade, so I asked Garcia to go check it out while I stayed near Sophia. I got another call about suspicious activity and left Sophia," Marco became quiet. "I was only gone a few minutes, but it was too late.

"It wasn't poison this time, but an impulsive murder. Perhaps Jax was triggered by Sophia. The situation got out of hand, and she paid the ultimate price - her sacrifice helped us, and I will never let this town forget that," Marco vowed, his chin quivering.

"He told me he was going back home to drop off his work receipts..." Lola said in a low voice.

"The evidence I have, Garcia brought me. Jade...had it in her mouth, Lola. And it was this book," Marco said, taking Jax's book out of his briefcase - the same one he was carrying when he first entered her shop. "It has the step-by-step of each murder. Jax wanted to write a 'masterpiece,' as he put it. It has every haiku, every interview, every step of his plan, including the why. He named his work: 'The Art of Murderous Poetry' and it's incomplete, thankfully."

"What do you mean?" Lola asked, meeting his gaze, then letting her eyes fall upon the book.

"Because you were the finale of his masterpiece. The book depicts how he framed you for everything and how, before you were arrested or taken away from him, you would be his only true sin. The haiku read:

"Two kindred souls born,

One is completely shattered,

And one fades away."

***

Are we really going? Jade asked. *He's spent over two and a half months in that solid rock.*

"Yes, Jade. Please give me back my ball of yarn, I need to add the finishing touch," replied Lola. She made a loop, pulled through, rounded the yarn, crocheted the close and saw that it was done. It was time.

When she arrived at the prison, her boyfriend Marco was waiting for her. He stayed with her until the very last moment. Jade, on the other hand, was on a leash, something new that Marco had suggested, and that Jade found fascinating, especially the custom-made harness and leash that were a striking emerald with genuine Swarovski crystals around the collar. Jade looked regal. Her comments about the smells of the place and how empty it looked without cats were ironically comforting to Lola.

Once she was alone in the cold, stale room, Jax entered, handcuffed. He had lost some weight, Lola noticed. Jade sneezed. He shuffled forward and sat in front of her, he tried to say something, but she raised a hand to silence him.

She reached down into her bag and pulled out the sweater.

"Take this sweater I crocheted for you. I used the new technique I told you about. the darn sleeve was a pickle, but I fixed it," Lola chuckled, stifling back tears, patting the sweater, picking off some lent. "I hope you like it," Lola said quietly.

"Lola, *why*?" Jax asked, tears running down his face, staring at the intricately detailed, full sweater. It looked like it should be sold in a high-end retail store on the mainland.

Up until this point, she had avoided eye contact, but she raised her gaze, her matching emerald eyes, wet with tears, held Jax's gaze for a few seconds before answering:

"Because my work is complete."

THE END.

***

What did you think of this book? Did you love it and want to read more?
Then you'll LOVE Monkey Business & Murder**.**

It's a book about...Avery Jensen, owner of a cozy B&B, enlists the help of her mischievous *and naughty* capuchin monkey to uncover small town secrets and long-buried family rivalries. Read Chapter One on the very next page!

SNEAK PEEK

Monkey Business & Murder Sneak Peek

———

Some monkeys can't help it, they *just* have to steal people's jewelry...or their murder weapon.

Avery is shocked to find a dead body on the festival grounds rather than the monkey's favorite sticky caramel apples when a former resident turns up dead at a local fall festival.

Avery Jensen, owner of a cozy B&B, enlists the help of her mischievous *and naughty* capuchin monkey to uncover small town secrets and long-buried family rivalries.

This picturesque small town in the mountains, where fall festivals are a must-attend event for the close-knit community, was the last place to harbor a double murder...*or was it?*

Armed with her nosy nature and a monkey with a taste for theft, Avery sets out to unravel the tangled webs of secrets and lies that led to this tragedy. As she digs deeper, she discovers that the town's dark secrets run deep and that some folks will go to deadly lengths to keep them buried once and for all.

With the monkey's kleptomaniac tendencies leading to unexpected clues and a killer on the loose, the duo embarks on a perilous journey in order to discover the killer's deadly secrets before it is too late.

CHAPTER ONE

"Hey, Avery?"

Avery turned from the canvas. A splotch of red paint dropped from the brush and onto the already paint-splattered floor.

A pretty girl with sleek black hair and a sweet face was poking her head through the door.

"What's up?"

"Could you come check this guy in?" Meihui asked.

Avery raised an eyebrow. "Isn't that your job?"

"I know, but…" Meihui looked back over her shoulder, then turned to Avery again, lowering her voice. "There's something weird about him. He creeps me out."

"Meihui. It takes five minutes to check someone in. You'll be fine."

Meihui made a face, muttered something that sounded like, "Ugh, *fine*," under her breath, and vanished from the doorway.

Avery rolled her eyes and turned back toward the canvas where she had made a grand total of three brushstrokes. She wasn't even sure what, exactly, she was painting, and now that Meihui had mentioned something strange about the customer, she couldn't focus on painting at all.

Sighing, Avery dropped the brush in a cup of water and stood to go make sure Meihui wasn't just being… well, Meihui. As she approached the counter, her eyes narrowed, and she actually saw what her employee meant and had to agree. Something was off here.

Avery squinted at the man hunched over the guest sign-in book. When he straightened, a prickling feeling grew at the back of her head, prodding her. She wasn't sure if it was the brown curls or the shape of his blue eyes, but there was something about him.

"I'm sorry," she said. "But, have you stayed here before?"

The man—Scott Johnson, according to the sign-in sheet—frowned, his lips turning pencil-thin.

"No," he said. Something flickered behind his eyes.

"Sorry," Avery said, putting on her best 'customer service' smile. "You just look really familiar, that's all."

Scott Johnson shrugged. "I just have one of those faces."

"What brings you to Brook Acres?"

"Business," came his reply. He was trying to be dismissive, which honestly just annoyed Avery and made her try even harder to engage him in conversation. She checked the reservation. "It says you're here for a week? Then you'll be in town for the Falling Leaf Festival next week, it's a—"

"Yearly festival slash farmer's market that has hay rides and carnival games and funnel cakes and all sorts of other fun things," the man finished.

"You've been here before then? Maybe that's how I—"

"I haven't." He cut her off rather abruptly and curtly. Then he took a deep breath as though to compose himself. "I haven't. But all festivals this time of year are like that, especially in charming little towns like this. I'm sorry, but I really want to get some rest. Which room is mine?"

"You'll have—"

But her words were cut off when a bright chirrup came from the ceiling. Avery, Meihui, and Scott Johnson all looked up.

"Is that a—?" But he didn't finish his question as the capuchin monkey clambered down from where it had been sitting on his favorite perch to jump onto Avery's shoulder.

"Sorry about that," Avery said, scratching the monkey's neck. "Ali here just likes to say 'hi' to new guests."

Ali chirruped again and hopped onto the reception desk, nudging the guestbook to the ground with a thunk. Ali looked down at the book, then back at Avery, looking a little chagrined.

"I...see." Scott watched as the capuchin jumped down from the desk, picked up the guest book, and handed it to Avery.

"As I was saying," Avery said, putting the book back on the counter. "You'll be in room three. It's the second floor, first door on the left once you get to the hallway."

She opened a drawer and rifled through until she came to a golden key with a large tag with the number '3' on it. Before she could hand it to Scott, however, Ali had hopped up and plucked the key from her hand. He gave a wide grin as he tried to scamper off with his new prize.

"Nope." Avery lunged, scooping the monkey into her arms. He made a sound of protest as she gently pried the key out of his little black fingers. "These are for our new friend. You have your own."

It was true. Once Avery had learned that Ali *really* liked shiny things—well, he liked anything that wasn't tied down—she had given him a few spare keys, hoping he would stop trying to steal the ones for the guests.

It hadn't worked.

"Here you are," she said, handing the key over to Scott while still holding Ali in her free arm. "Enjoy your stay. There's breakfast from seven until nine, and dinner from six until—"

"Thanks." Without ceremony, Scott took his suitcase and briefcase and headed up stairs.

"See what I mean?" Meihui hissed as soon as they heard the door slam shut up ahead. "He's creepy."

"Yes, and thank you so much for trying to pawn him off on me."

Meihui rolled her eyes. She might have said something else, but the phone rang right at that moment. Sighing, the young girl picked up the phone.

"Mountain Acres Bed and Breakfast, this is Meihui speaking. How may I help you?"

Avery smiled and went back into her office. Meihui loved to complain, but she was a good employee at heart. And, though Avery wouldn't admit it, the twenty-something-year-old had a knack for noticing something off about a guest. She had pointed out the woman who had tried to break into Avery's room and steal her jewelry as soon as she stepped into the Bed and Breakfast, and she'd been right about the young man who came in with his wife a few months ago. They'd had to call the police that time. There was something about Scott Johnson that wasn't right either.

With that in mind, she went to her computer and pulled up his reservation. It had been made through Grim Peters' travel agency, so he had paid through there, instead of paying the B&B directly. That wasn't unusual, and Grim usually recommended Mountain Acres to out of towners. She usually got at least five bookings a month through her. Grim hadn't messaged her telling her to watch out, which she had done once or twice. Thankfully, Grim didn't have the same intuition as Meihui, and there hadn't been any incidents there.

So why did this man bother her so much?

Honestly, it might have just been the way he was a bit rude. Brook Acres had had its share of "Yankees" come through, mostly around the fall or spring, so the slightly blunter personalities didn't bother her too much. It wasn't that there was anything wrong with people up north; she actually liked them quite a bit. They just moved at a faster pace than people in a small town in the Appalachians. She wondered if he was from New York, or Massachusetts.

Except, as she combed through the reservation, she saw he wasn't from the Northeast at all. He was from Pigeon Forge, Tennessee. At that distance, they were practically neighbors.

Maybe that was why he looked so familiar, she thought. He'd been here before. Maybe he had family in town, or maybe in Boone. They sometimes got people who had kids at App State who wanted to stay outside of Boone if it was particularly busy that weekend.

Why had he been so hostile, though, if either of those were the case?

She was still contemplating this when she heard a cheerful chattering sound and a familiar weight pushed down on her left shoulder.

"Hi, Ali," she said, reaching up to scratch the back of his neck. Ali leaned his head against hers for a brief moment before hopping down. He managed to hop on the keyboard, and a long string of gibberish ran across the search bar. She was about to pull him off when she noticed something clasped in his hands, which he was holding suspiciously close to his chest, as though he were trying to hide it from her.

"Give it here," she said, sticking out her hand. Ali held whatever-it-was closer and turned his body slightly away from her. "Ali..."

When she reached out and pried the monkey's little black fingers away, he released the watch he'd been holding with a tiny chirrup of protest.

"At least this one is mine," she said, tucking it in her pocket.

Ali looked like a normal capuchin: a white face and biceps, and black everywhere else. But he'd always been a bit peculiar ever since Avery had gotten him five years ago. She'd read that monkeys were notoriously difficult to keep, but that hadn't been the case with Ali. He was intelligent, docile, and even housetrained. She had set him up a giant play area in the expansive backyards and into the woods beyond, but he never strayed far. He loved Avery, and she loved him.

"Come on." Avery scooped Ali up into her arms. "Let's go clean the dining room."

As she cleaned and got ready for dinner, all she could think about was Scott Johnson. She definitely knew him from somewhere, and she was determined to figure out from where.

To continue reading Monkey Business & Murder go to: www.amaz on.com/dp/B0C7FC6CTC and grab the book!.

Printed in Great Britain
by Amazon